COMPARTMENTS

Zoran Živković

Compartments

FG-RS0006L3
ISBN: 978-4-908793-16-5

Cover: Youchan Ito, Togoru Art Works

Neoclassic Fleurons font used with permission of
Paulo W–Intellecta Design

Cadmus Press
cadmusmedia.org

COMPARTMENTS

Zoran Živković

Translated from the Serbian
by
Alice Copple-Tošić

Cadmus Press
2018

Contents

1. Compartments

I RAN AS FAST as my legs would carry me.

The carriage had just pulled away from the buffer at the end of the track. Even though it was still moving slowly, had I been carrying any luggage, particularly anything heavy, I wouldn't have made it. Luckily, all I was holding was my coat and hat.

I didn't know how to get onto a moving carriage. Was I first supposed to jump onto the step on the platform of the last car and then grab hold of the handrail, or the other way around? Who knows what I would have done if the back door hadn't opened just as I caught up to the car. The conductor came out onto the platform.

"Give me your hand!" he shouted.

I stretched out the arm with my coat thrown over it. He grabbed my hand and heaved mightily. The next instant I was standing next to him on the platform.

"Wonderful!" said the conductor with a smile.

"I'm sorry," I replied, out of breath.

"Come, now! You have no reason to excuse yourself. Quite the contrary. I'm delighted that you joined us. Welcome!"

He patted me lightly on the shoulder. We stood there for several moments without speaking, smiling at each other.

"I'm afraid I don't have a ticket," I said contritely.

"The ticket isn't important. The essential thing is that you made it."

"I'm extremely grateful to you."

"Let's go in," said the conductor, moving aside to let me enter first.

I went inside the car. He came in after me, closed the door and then locked it. Turning towards me, he held out both his hands.

"Please let me take your coat and hat."

"Oh," I said, and gave them to him.

The conductor opened a narrow closet in the wall next to the rear door. It was full of overcoats, fur coats, mackintoshes, capes, ski jackets and windcheaters. The shelf above it held all kinds of hats and caps. There were shawls, gloves and muffs and three or four umbrellas too. He took a wooden hanger and hung my coat on it, then placed my hat on a free spot in the corner of the shelf. Then he bent down and took a pair of slippers with large pink pom-poms out of the lower part of the closet. That's when I noticed the shoes neatly placed on the floor: they were mostly ordinary shoes of different shapes and sizes, but there were a few pairs of sandals, boots, trainers, galoshes, clogs and thongs.

The conductor put the slippers on the dark-red carpet runner in front of me and then said, still bent over, "Your shoes, if you please."

I squatted down to untie my shoelaces. I pulled on the slippers as the conductor put my shoes away in the closet. We stood up simultaneously. Suddenly he began to stagger. His hands flew to his forehead and he leaned his back against the closet.

"Aren't you feeling well?" I asked anxiously.

"No, no, everything's all right," he said in a weary voice. "Just a little dizzy spell. It will soon pass."

The conductor was a tall, broad-shouldered man with bushy eyebrows, and this infirmity seemed unsuited to his size. He soon regained his composure, just as he'd predicted.

"Excuse me."

"Do you have low blood pressure? I've heard that people with low blood pressure feel dizzy when they stand up quickly."

The conductor's reply was not immediate. "It's not from low blood pressure," he said at last. "Whenever I close the closet, I remember. . . ."

He didn't finish the sentence. The smile of a moment before turned into a painful frown. I thought I should say something, but didn't know what.

"All of that has nothing to do with you, of course," he continued. "Why should you be interested in my feelings? I wouldn't blame you in the slightest if you told me my past has nothing to do with you and I mustn't bore you with it."

"Quite the contrary," I hastened to assure him. "I would love to hear it, if that will make you feel better. . . ."

"Oh, it will, it will!" His face lit up at once. "How kind of you. Such thoughtfulness is a rare thing nowadays. People are no longer sympathetic to the misfortunes of others. They don't have time for them. And sometimes all it takes is a little attention to help those near and dear to you." He paused for a moment and placed his hand on my shoulder. "Thank you!"

"Think nothing of it. . . ."

We regarded each other briefly, then he removed his hand from my shoulder.

"She was standing exactly where you are now." His voice altered to a deep, slow drawl. "When she took off her square-toed white leather pumps with silver buckles and stood on the runner in her stocking feet, virtually barefoot, I felt as though I'd been struck by lightning. Have you ever felt anything like that?"

"I've never been struck by lightning."

"Too bad. It's hard to imagine if it hasn't happened to you. I was bending over, giving her some slippers, just as I gave them to you a moment ago. I barely kept my balance. Although quite improper and strictly against the rules of service, I simply couldn't take my eyes off her calves. She was wearing a rather long skirt, but even so the little bit I could see was enough to make me throw all caution to the wind."

He stopped speaking and his gaze seemed to wander off somewhere. I waited patiently for it to return.

"She must have understood what was going on, because why else would she just stand there while my eyes shamelessly devoured her legs? She didn't accept the slippers I offered, and she could have. In fact, common decency required it of her. The comportment of a lady, if nothing else. But no, she chose to give herself up to my lustful eyes. I would even dare to say, although it might be too strong a word—that she surrendered. You won't reproach me, I hope, for this unbecoming description?"

"I won't."

"I don't know how long we stayed there like that, motionless, I bending over and she shoeless. It must have been a long time. If someone had happened along, it would have been a pretty sight to see. But no one appeared, which was unfortunate, because it might have broken the spell. I might have still had a chance to come to my senses. Although . . . may I be frank with you?"

"You may."

"It was already too late. I was beyond rescue. She and I both knew it. . . ."

He broke into a sob and covered his eyes with his left hand. Crying suited this large, mature man even less than the infirmity that had just overcome him. Once again I wasn't sure what to do.

"Then what happened?" I asked softly.

He didn't reply at once. He took a large white monogrammed handkerchief out of the breast pocket of his conductor's uniform, wiped his eyes with it and then blew his nose.

"Pardon me," he said in a voice that still trembled. "What happened next was inevitable. She extended her right foot towards me. The worst thing is that I didn't hesitate at all. Not a moment. I who am so proud of my common sense and self-control. I put the slipper on her foot, although regulations strictly forbid it. Yes, that's what I did. Don't be the least surprised."

"I'm not surprised."

"Naturally, I had to touch her foot. Just lightly, but that was enough for lightning to strike me again. She took no notice of my trembling and extended her left foot without hesitation. Many would see that as female frivolity, even shamelessness, but I accepted her foot without a second thought. Embraced it, you might even say. In any case, I held it longer than the time needed to put on the slipper. She didn't object. She serenely consented to let her tiny foot stay in my huge hand. In this."

He held out his right hand, palm up. We looked at it for several moments in silence, as though it still held signs of her foot. Finally, he clenched his hand into a fist and shook his head.

"What happened next, although dreadful, was bound to happen. You'll be horrified when I tell you. You might even be disgusted with me. I'm perfectly aware of the fact that I deserve the deepest scorn."

"Come now, . . ." I protested, on his falling silent.

"No, you mustn't be kind. I don't deserve it. I'm responsible for everything. I should have held back. Regardless of the cost. I was spellbound, that's true. I had lost control of myself, that's also true. But is that any justification? Are those extenuating circumstances? You be the judge."

"It would be easier to make a judgment if I knew what happened."

"Can't you guess?"

"I'm afraid not."

He stared at me in disbelief. Then he bowed his head and gazed fixedly at his hands, which he was now rubbing together.

"I kissed her left foot," he said almost in a whisper.

"Oh," escaped before I could stop it.

"It wasn't any kind of passionate kiss, of course," he hastened to add. "I barely lowered my lips. On the top, by her toes. Over her stockings. I managed at least that much self-restraint."

"I see," came my reply, since nothing better crossed my mind.

"There, now you know. It must be clear to you that I am beyond redemption."

"But . . ."

"Please, no," he said, interrupting me. "There's nothing you can say that will lessen my guilt. I have to live with my damnation. Don't waste your words. It's enough that you took the time to listen to me. You are a splendid chap."

"Thank you, although . . ."

"Let's not talk about me anymore. I've already taken up too much of your time with my problems. You aren't here to listen to the lamentations of ill-fated conductors. Are your slippers comfortable?"

I looked at my feet. "Yes, they are."

"Wonderful. Then let's go. If you please."

He passed me and turned left. I followed him. The corridor was wide and lined with the same carpet runner as the entrance to the car. All the windows on the right-hand side were covered with long, pleated velvet curtains, also dark red. Five-branched candelabras lighted the entrance to each of the six compartments. The candle flames burned without flickering.

The conductor stopped at the first compartment. He took off his hat, put it under his arm, smoothed his hair, then knocked on the glassed-in section of the door. A curtain identical to the one on the window opposite it hid the interior from view.

Some time passed before a woman's small voice was heard from the compartment. "Come in."

The conductor gave me a brief, indecisive look before he pulled the sliding door aside and moved the curtain slightly, just enough to stick his head inside.

"I am pleased to inform you that we have a new passenger. The gentleman is very polished and full of compassion. I thought you might enjoy his company."

Quite a while passed before the same woman's voice replied, "It will be our pleasure."

The conductor withdrew his head, grinned at me, then pulled back the curtain and gestured toward the interior with his hand.

I stopped at the entrance to the compartment. On the left, next to the door, sat a plump, balding man in a three-piece suit, with reading glasses halfway down his nose. His hands were busy knitting. A bright yellow scarf cascaded down from large knitting needles. The place next to his was empty, and beside the window (with the curtain drawn) was a tiny middle-aged woman dressed in black. The hat she was wearing was also black and had a lace veil that covered half her face. In her hands was an open book, small but thick, with a dark cover. On the right sat three young girls aged ten or eleven. They were wearing identical sailor suits, white knee socks and patent leather shoes. Long braids dangled below their caps and their faces were exactly similar.

I nodded and said, "Hello. Thank you for being so kind as to let me join you."

Four pairs of eyes looked at me. Only the man kept his eyes fixed on his knitting.

"Come in," said the woman in black at last in a squeaky voice, giving a curt nod in return. She indicated the empty seat next to her.

As soon as I entered the compartment, there came from behind me the sound of curtains moving and the sliding door closing. I sat down and folded my hands in my lap. My eyes were drawn to the large chandelier hanging directly under the compartment's high ceiling. The five candles on it were not real; frosted light bulbs shaped like flames brightly lit the interior.

I kept my eyes trained upward until the thin voice addressed me once more. "You are undoubtedly wondering why I'm wearing black."

I turned to my left. "No, I . . ."

"Let me tell you right away," she continued. "I'm in mourning for my late husband. There he is, over there."

She bent forward a bit and nodded in the direction of the man and his knitting. I turned towards him. He just sat there, deeply absorbed in his work. But his movements became a bit livelier.

"Mama," said the girl sitting in the middle.

The lady looked at her sharply from under her veil. The girl quickly lowered her head and the other two did the same in unison.

"He might not look dead," continued the woman, "but don't let appearances deceive you. He's dead as far as I'm concerned."

She lowered the book into her lap and took a small black handkerchief out of her left sleeve. She slipped it under her veil and dabbed at the corners of her eyes, then returned it to her sleeve.

"He was a wonderful man. An exemplary husband, a caring and gentle father. He devoted all his free time to his daughters, teaching them different skills that young girls need to know, acting in particular. You'd never think he'd stoop so low. And right in front of his children. Isn't it just awful?"

"I wouldn't know. . . ."

"But you have every right to know. I will tell you everything, then you can decide for yourself."

"Mama," said the girl next to the window without lifting her head.

The woman raised her veil and shot a piercing glance with tiny black eyes.

"Apple!" she said brusquely.

"Not apples! Please! Anything but that!" replied the girl, terrified.

"All three!"

"No, Mama!" cried the other two girls in harmony.

"At once!" hissed the woman.

The girl in the middle quickly reached into the deep pocket of her skirt and took out three apples wrapped in white napkins. She handed one to each sister. With trembling fingers they unwrapped the large, green fruit. They didn't start eating right away but looked pleadingly at their mother. The woman's expression was unrelenting. They sighed as they bit into the apples.

"I certainly must seem too strict to you," said the woman, turning to me once again, "but now that I'm a widow, I have no choice. All the responsibility for raising my daughters lies with me. Should I let them degenerate like their father?"

"No, of course not," I said, shaking my head.

"After hearing what happened, you might lay some of the blame on her. Perhaps all the blame. You might think that he is merely the innocent victim of a cunning seductress. But it's not like that. No one can be seduced against his will, correct? Why didn't anyone seduce me like that?"

"Seductress?"

"I had a feeling something bad was about to happen as soon as I saw the conductor all wide-eyed when he came to ask us if we would take her into our compartment. I don't doubt in the least that she'd bewitched him beforehand. He seemed confused, even stunned. You must know what a man looks like when he's in the grip of a certain kind of woman?"

"I can imagine. . . ."

"There, you see. I was just about to say that we were unable to accommodate anyone else, but my husband prevented me. I was so amazed I was speechless. He'd always left such decisions up to me before. It's only natural, wouldn't you say?"

"Without a doubt."

"He said it would be an honor to have her join us. Just imagine—an honor!"

I shook my head.

"I had a fresh slight waiting for me when she came in. She simply sat down where you are sitting now. Without a word of gratitude. As if that place belonged to her by birthright. She didn't even look at me, as though I wasn't in the compartment. She held her head high, flaunting and haughty. And then her scent hit me."

"Scent?" I repeated inquiringly, since the lady had broken off.

"Cloying, aggressive. Depraved. You know who uses such scent."

"Do you mean . . . ?"

"Please, we aren't alone." She nodded her head towards the girls, who were tearfully eating their apples.

"Oh, of course. Excuse me."

"We all realized right away what we were dealing with, but did he as the father of the family do anything about it? If not out of respect for his wife, then at least for the sake of his young daughters? He should have ordered her to leave at once, that would have been the only way to redeem himself at least in part for having so recklessly let her enter. But he didn't. He didn't throw her out, and then he had the gall to strike up a conversation with her. Lascivious, promiscuous small talk, actually. Within our earshot. As I watched our girls blush in embarrassment, I wanted to sink through the floor."

"Is that possible?" I turned towards the man engrossed in his knitting.

"Yes, quite so. And do you know what they were allegedly talking about?"

"No."

"The weather."

"The weather?"

"That's right. The hot sun, swollen clouds, humid air, raging storms."

"What's that you're saying?"

"Yes. As if we were ignorant fools who couldn't grasp what they were really talking about."

"Unbelievable."

"Unbelievable, yes. But just wait until you hear what happened next."

I waited. The lady looked at me meaningfully several moments before she said, "He offered her apples."

"Apples?" I gestured towards the girls.

"Yes. The same apples that these poor things now have to eat. I thought I would faint when I heard it."

I shook my head.

"And if you'd only seen how lustfully he looked at her as she bit into the apple! As I'm sure you are aware, fruit is very juicy, but she paid no attention whatsoever to that fact. She let the juice dribble out of the corners of her mouth and run down her chin. Then he took out a handkerchief and wiped the juice. Before my very own eyes. And she let him do it, calm as you please. With an impish grin. She even turned toward me briefly and gave a defiant look."

The lady raised the back of her left hand to her forehead and bowed her head dramatically. The girls across from her sniffled in unison.

"How was I to know," she continued after a short pause, "that this was just an inoffensive prelude to what would happen in the tunnel?"

"Mama," mumbled the girl next to the door, her mouth full.

"Quiet!" said the woman sharply, silencing her. "Even though it is our shame, there's no reason to hide it. Let everyone know what your father was like. The fact that he is now dead doesn't mitigate his guilt one bit."

The girl in the middle raised her head. It looked as if she were going to protest, but then she lowered her head again and continued eating her apple.

"As you know," said the woman, continuing our conversation, "when the carriage enters a tunnel all light disappears. We are in the pitch black. And right then, as she so ceremoniously ate the apple, he her willing assistant, we went into a tunnel. It was the worst thing that could have happened. I don't like tunnels in the best of circumstances and I went numb with fear. If this was how he acted while we were watching him, what would he do when we couldn't see?"

Just as she said this, we were plunged into darkness. A tiny hand dropped gently onto my left knee.

"It was just like this. You surely feel uncomfortable too, don't you?"

"Well, a little, yes."

Her hand squeezed a bit harder. "Don't be afraid. This tunnel is short, the light will soon return. But at that time, unfortunately, it was very long. Long enough for him to tell her the whole story."

"Story?"

"Yes. The story of the wax button. Our most intimate secret. Until that moment no one knew about it except the two of us. It should have stayed that way. We should have taken it to the grave with us. But he divulged it to her shamelessly. To me he died, completely and irrevocably, before the light returned."

A quiet cough came out of the darkness to my right. I turned that way, even though I couldn't see anything.

The little fingers seemed to dig into my knee, so I quickly turned back around.

"Don't pay any attention to him. He's trying to arouse your pity. He expects you to feel sorry for him because he's dead. But he doesn't deserve your pity, not at all."

The pressure from her fingers was suddenly released.

"Or maybe you think otherwise?"

"I wouldn't know. . . ."

"Perhaps you think that what he did wasn't so terrible? That I was unmerciful?"

"No, actually. . . ."

"Perhaps you even think that I'm to blame for everything, that he is only an innocent victim of my callousness?"

"Certainly not, of course. . . ."

The tiny hand removed itself from my knee and the chandelier lights went on the same moment.

The woman once again took her handkerchief out of her sleeve, but this time she only twisted it in her lap. The girls had stopped eating their apples and were staring at us fixedly.

"I was wrong about you," she said in a choking voice. "I believed you to be a true gentleman."

"But . . ."

"It serves me right for being so easily fooled. I clearly should have been suspicious right away, as soon as the conductor put in a good word for you. Polished and full of compassion—indeed!"

"I assure you . . ."

"Please, not another word," she said sharply, interrupting me. "Have at least a little consideration for the children. There's nothing more to say, in any case. Everything is quite clear."

She rummaged for a moment through the black handbag between us, then took out a silver bell and rang it. Almost the same instant the door slid open and the conductor's head poked through the curtain.

"The gentleman will be leaving us," she said in an authoritative voice. The conductor pulled the curtain aside without hesitation and I stood up. I stopped at the door and turned around. The father was still engrossed in his knitting and the mother had returned to her book. Only the girls looked at me as they continued to bite into their apples. Their chins were wet from the juice. Not knowing what to say as I left, I merely nodded briefly and went out into the corridor. The conductor quickly pulled the curtain shut behind me and closed the door.

We stood for a moment facing each other in silence. Then he took a pair of manicure scissors out of the right breast pocket of his uniform.

"Please, allow me."

He took hold of my left hand and started to trim my nails, starting with the thumb.

"That was a mistake, of course," he said when he reached the middle finger. "I shouldn't have taken you into their compartment. But all one can do is hope. I thought that things might have changed. I was waiting here in front of the door and the silence was encouraging. I'd started to believe that things would be different this time, and then I heard the bell. I feel very embarrassed. Please forgive me."

"I don't blame you for anything. . . ."

Before he moved to my right hand, he put the clipped nails in his pocket, then looked me straight in the eye.

"You talked about her, didn't you? I can only imagine what the woman said. But you mustn't believe her.

Please, I implore you. She doesn't like her. Actually, it's even worse, she hates her. Although there's absolutely no reason, of course. She accuses her of something that is entirely not her fault. She's not the reason that the woman is a widow. The woman herself is to blame for that."

This time he started with the pinky.

"By the way, just between you and me, his death is rather suspicious. All right, he might act like he's defunct, but that doesn't prove a thing. What if she changes her mind and orders him to stop knitting? It wouldn't surprise me in the least. She's liable to do anything. Then what?"

He raised his eyes to mine. I shrugged my shoulders.

"Did she mention a button?" he asked quietly, after hesitating a bit, concentrating on the hangnail on my index finger.

I answered with a nod, although his eyes were lowered and he couldn't see it.

"A wax button?"

"Yes," I said.

"Let me clue you in."

He didn't do it right away, though. He put the manicure scissors back in his pocket along with the newly clipped nails, took out a nail file and got down to work.

"She lied to you," he said after finishing three fingers on my left hand.

"Is that so?" I replied, surprised.

"It wasn't made of real wax at all."

"It wasn't?"

He raised my finished hand up high, blew on it, polished the nails a bit, then took my right hand.

"It wasn't," he continued after finishing my ring finger, "but I'm not at liberty to say anything else, unfortunately. I've already told you too much. It might cost me my job. You won't report me, I trust?"

He stopped filing and looked at me imploringly. I hastened to reassure him.

"Heaven forbid."

His face lit up. "I knew I could trust you."

Since my other hand was now polished and inspected, he nodded in satisfaction. "There. Now everything's in order. How do you feel?"

I spread out the fingers of both hands and looked at them. "Fine," I said. "Quite fine."

"Wonderful. Shall we continue, then?"

He put it in the form of a question, but didn't await my reply. He placed the file back in his pocket, turned and headed for the entrance to the second compartment.

He halted in front of it, turned towards me and signaled with his hand that I should stop, although I hadn't moved at all. He opened the door quickly and slipped through the curtains, then closed the door behind him.

He remained inside for a short time. When he emerged he was smiling ear to ear.

"The brothers will receive you. It is a rare honor. Please show due consideration for their rules of behavior."

"Certainly."

He moved aside but did not pull the curtains open. I slipped through them as he had a moment before and entered the compartment. From behind me came the sound of the door sliding shut.

Inside I found six monks. They were sitting pressed together on four seats, leaving two places empty next to the door. They were wearing long brown cowls and had white cords around their waists. One of them had his hood pulled down. He was sitting on the left next to the curtained window, head bowed, so I couldn't see his face. The attention of the other brothers was focused on him. All five were holding notebooks and writing something in them.

At first no one paid any attention to me. Finally, the closest monk on the right turned towards me and put his notebook in his lap. Just like the others, he had a smoothly shaved head and ruddy face. He put his hands over his ears and bowed to me. I returned the bow the same way. He indicated with a nod that I was to sit on the empty seat next to him. When I sat down, he raised his right index finger to his lips.

We looked at each other in silence for some time. Then he took his notebook, turned the page and started to write. When he had finished, he handed me the notebook.

Please forgive me for not being able to talk to you in the normal way. The members of our order have taken a vow of silence. But there are no restrictions as far as writing is concerned. You may speak to me by whispering in my ear.

I put my head close to his and whispered, "I am very honored by the fact that you have taken me into your compartment. I hope I won't be any bother."

The monk shook his head briskly, then set about writing in his notebook again. When he handed it to me, I saw that he'd written down my answer under his first message, and then his new words:

Do you play chess by any chance?

I didn't reply at once. His face was full of eagerness. I finally nodded.

The monk quickly scribbled: *Would you like a game?*

"Here? Now?" I asked in a whisper.

He quickly wrote his answer: *Yes. Yes.*

I thought it over briefly, then shrugged my shoulders. "Why not? If it won't disturb the brothers, of course." I motioned my head towards the monks engrossed in their writing.

On the contrary, came the new message. *They won't have anything against it. They love chess, too. It's our order's favorite game.*

"Then fine."

The monk smiled and clapped his hands. The brother with the hood pulled down over his face didn't move, but the other four stopped their writing and fixed inquisitive eyes on us.

My mute collocutor turned the page of his notebook, wrote something brief, and showed it to the brothers. When they read the message there was an instant uproar. First, almost all of them jumped up from their seats, clapped each other on the shoulder, and even hugged each other. The two of us stood up too. Then the monks went one by one to the monk next to me and kissed him on both cheeks and twice on the forehead. He stood there beaming with joy, his eyes closed. Finally, they all shook my hand firmly.

I was motioned to sit down again, and when I did so the monk I'd talked to moved to the seat across from me. One of the brothers knelt down on the dark red carpet runner and started to feel about under my seat. I raised my feet a bit to get out of his way. He pulled out a large chess set and handed it to my future opponent, but he didn't get up. He stayed on his hands and knees and moved back all the way to the door, taking up the space between us. The brother across from me opened the set, shook out the pieces on the closed notebook in his lap, then placed the board on the back of the monk on the floor.

He sorted through the pieces a bit and finally singled out two white pawns. He picked them up and showed them to everyone. Four heads nodded in confirmation. He put his hands behind his back and shifted the pawns about for a while. Then he brought his hands forward, clenched into fists, and held them out in front of me.

I thought of standing up and asking him in a whisper what choice there was between two pieces of the same color, but I was hemmed in. I didn't know if I would be able to sit down afterwards. In any case, it made no difference. After thinking it over briefly, I pointed to his left hand. It opened, and everyone clapped upon seeing the white pawn.

Two of the monks squeezed in between the chess player and the brother with the hood pulled down over his face. The third sat on the floor in front of the one who'd loaned us his back for a table. He quickly began to set up the pieces. But he didn't set them in their starting positions and he didn't use all the pieces. When he had finished, he moved back a little. All I needed was a cursory glance at the board to realize that before me was an endgame. The black king was in checkmate. I looked inquisitively at the brother on the seat across from me and shrugged my shoulders.

He took his notebook, wrote something in it and handed it to me. The message was short: *Your move.*

I pointed at the pen in his hand. When he gave it to me, I wrote in the next empty line: *But the game is over.*

He did not reply at once. First he showed the four observers my message in the notebook, to which they bowed deeply. Then he started to write again:

On the contrary, went his new message. *It has yet to begin. The rules of our order dictate that we play chess from checkmate back to the opening positions.*

I looked at him for several moments, then gave him back his notebook and stared at the pieces on the board. But I didn't have time to evaluate the situation there, because the lights suddenly went out.

A stir broke out that same moment in the darkness. There was the rustling of cowls and then the sound of pieces flying in all directions. A voice from the side opposite me said in haste, "Get up, quick!"

I wasn't sure whether this was directed at me, but I obeyed. As I stood up I collided with someone. I wanted to excuse myself, but there was no time, because that was when the singing started.

The darkness of the compartment was filled with a woman's voice. The soprano emanated from where the monk was sitting with his hood drawn over his face. I tried to see through the murk to that side, but to no avail. The song was slow, almost dreamy, in a language I didn't understand, full of open vowels. It sounded like a dirge. I couldn't tell how it affected the monks, but it filled me at once with excitement. When it finished, it left behind the bitter feeling of something withheld.

Silence reigned for a while, and then the male voice of a moment before spoke again.

"That is her present to our brother."

"I thought . . ." I started in a whisper, but I didn't finish.

"The vow of silence does not hold in a tunnel, you can speak freely in a normal voice."

"Oh, I see."

"We do not normally receive women into our company when we are not properly dressed—you cannot see, but we are wearing slippers instead of clogs under our robes. Nonetheless, our brother invited her in. He had the right by seniority. When she came in, she paid no attention to the others. She headed straight for him and sat in his lap. First she only looked into his eyes, holding his hands, then she started whispering to him. This lasted for some time. All he did was nod his head. After she'd finished, she simply got up and left. Without a word. She didn't play a single game of chess."

"Not a single game?"

"Not a single game, but she made up for it. You heard the song."

"It's captivating."

"It's more than that. Do you know what it's about?"

"No."

"A horned egg!"

"Really?"

"Yes, but he doesn't recount the story all at once, of course. It wouldn't be possible, after all. It's a good thing our brother only sings in tunnels, so there are breathing spells. Otherwise he wouldn't be able to keep it up. Singing in a woman's voice is very taxing."

"I would imagine so."

"The rest of us welcome the breaks too. So we can write down what we've heard. It's immensely important."

"Quite so."

"We will have to get down to work as soon as we come out of the tunnel. Please forgive us for not being able to finish the game. It is indeed a pity, because the position was quite challenging."

"Think nothing of it."

"We'll make up for the loss the next time you visit us. Please drop by at any time."

"With pleasure."

"Then goodbye."

"Goodbye."

I stood there in the darkness. Incoherent chatter filled the compartment, punctuated by a giggle and coughing here and there. Someone's hands suddenly covered my ears. They didn't remain there long, but soon came back, a total of five times. It was only afterwards that I realized that it had been a different pair of hands each time. Immediately after the last salutation the door behind my back opened and something slipped through the curtains. I felt a hand take hold of my arm and lead me out. The next moment I was in the corridor.

"Aren't they wonderful?" said the conductor. A large white towel was thrown over his left arm and the small table next to him bore a little dish with a bar of wet soap, a brush, a razor and a hand mirror in a silver frame.

"Yes, they're pleasantly gregarious," I replied.

"Allow me." He took me by the shoulders and set me under the candelabrum by the door. He shook out the towel, tucked it into my shirt collar, and spread it out so it covered my entire chest. Then he took the little dish and brush and with brisk movements began whipping the soap into a foam.

"I'll let you in on a secret," he said as he started daubing the white foam on my face. "I pray that I may?"

"Of course."

He leaned toward me confidentially. "Whenever I get the chance, I stand in front of their door when we're in a tunnel and I eavesdrop."

He stepped back, inspected me, removed a bit a foam from under my nose with his finger and wiped it on the towel.

"I can't hear all that well, but it's enough. I get goose bumps every time. Her voice is angelic, isn't it?"

"Yes, it's divine."

"Listening through the door has its advantages. You don't see who's singing and it's easy to imagine that it really is her inside. Even though I know it isn't, unfortunately. . . ."

He brought the hand with the brush to his mouth and bit the knuckle of his index finger. He stood there like that without moving, looking through me with sorrowful eyes.

"Forgive me," he said, snapping out of his trance.

"Think nothing of it."

"It's hard, you know. . . ."

"I know."

"But life goes on. What's to be done?"

He set the dish and brush on the table. He unbuttoned the upper part of his uniform, then took off his belt. He handed me the end with the buckle.

"Hold onto it firmly, please."

He grabbed hold of the other end of the belt and stepped back to the window, tightening it. Then he took the razor from the table, opened it, and started to draw the flat side over the belt, stropping the blade first on one side and then on the other.

"There's only one thing I don't like about the monks."

"Oh, and what is that?"

"That ruse about choosing black or white chess pieces. Yes, that's what it is. I won't shrink at all from calling a spade a spade. A ruse. They know it's dishonest, but they resort to it just the same. You're lucky you didn't play a match."

"How do you know I didn't?"

"It would be quite obvious if you had. Your head would be shaved, just like theirs."

"Why?"

"Didn't they tell you? They've really become deceitful. That's the bet. That's what you play for."

"What if I'd won? What would be my prize? They don't have anything to shave."

"They would have to let their hair grow, and that would be much harder for them than it would be for you to have your head shaved. You hair would grow back, while they would no longer have the right to cut their hair. But they were in no danger of losing. They are true masters at backwards chess. They've only lost once so far. She beat them."

"She? But they told me she didn't play at all."

"They told you that? Liars! They're trying to cover their shame. She not only beat them, she completely outplayed them."

He looked left and right down the corridor, then drew close to me, loosening the belt.

"Why do you think the brother who sings has his hood on?" he asked in a low voice.

"I have no idea."

"So you can't see his hair," he continued in a whisper. "It's all grown out. But he won't be able to use his hood much longer. When his hair grows a bit longer he won't be able to hide it. We'll just see what they do then."

He laid the razor on the table, put on his belt, and buttoned his uniform. Then he took up the razor once again and started to shave me. His movements were light and skillful. I barely felt the touch of the blade.

He finished the left side of my face before speaking again.

"Ha, if I could only tell you what I know about the horned egg. Then none of it would look quite so idyllic. But I mustn't. I'm sure you wouldn't give me away, but that's not the point. I don't want to get either one of us into trouble. And it's far from minor, believe me. You have to treat the horned egg with cautious respect. Many have paid a high price for being caught off-guard. You don't want to come to unnecessary harm, do you?"

As he was then shaving around my mouth, I couldn't take the risk of talking. I just mumbled something vague through closed lips.

"It's a real joy to deal with a sensible man," he continued. "That is a rare virtue nowadays. People generally act foolishly, even when I warn them about what's awaiting them. Curiosity blinds them completely. As if the world will go to ruin unless they know what's concealed behind the horned egg. They regret it afterwards, of course, but then it's too late."

He took a step backwards and began to inspect me. He nodded his head, then removed the towel and wiped my face with it. He placed the towel on the table, picked up the mirror and handed it to me.

"What do you say?"

I looked at myself.

"Perfect. Thank you."

"You're welcome. We couldn't have left that out. You can't go any further unless you're freshly shaved."

He went up to the door of the third compartment, adjusted his tie a bit, then knocked. He didn't employ a normal knock. First he knocked three times quickly, then two times slowly, then three times quickly again.

There was no immediate reply. The conductor turned briefly towards me and smiled in apology. Finally there came a knock from the compartment: three slow knocks, two fast, then three slow.

The conductor nodded with satisfaction and opened

the door. He pushed the curtain halfway open and indicated with his other hand that I was to go inside.

I went in and the door quickly closed behind me.

There were only two passengers in the compartment. A painter was sitting next to the covered window on the left with an easel that held a square canvas. He had a broad beret, a red scarf around his neck, and blue overalls smeared with paint here and there. His right hand held a wooden palette and his left hand a brush. He was wearing glasses with a round frame and opaque black lenses. An unlit pipe with a curved stem hung from his mouth.

A dwarf was lying on the middle seat opposite. He was wearing a turquoise leotard and pink ballet shoes. His body was very muscular, which made him asymmetrical. His legs were raised in the air and his feet supported a large purple ball.

"Undress," said the painter to me, not turning his head in my direction.

"Excuse me?" I asked in amazement.

"Undress, undress," repeated the dwarf.

"What in the world are you talking about?"

"How do you suppose I am to paint you if you don't undress?"

"Yes," said the dwarf like an echo, "how do you suppose, how do you suppose?"

"I don't suppose at all," I replied angrily.

"Then why did you come?"

"Yes, why, why?"

"I thought that . . ." I said, turning briefly towards the door. I wanted to mention the conductor, but couldn't find the right words.

"So now what?"

"What, what?"

"Maybe the best thing would be for me to leave?"

"Leave? Out of the question. Every person who enters here must be in the picture. You certainly must realize that."

"Certainly, certainly."

"I didn't know. . . ."

"So you won't undress?"

"Won't, won't?"

"I won't."

"How about part way?"

"Part way, part way?"

I shook my head.

"Just your pants?"

"Pants, pants?"

I shook my head even harder.

"All right, then at least your tie."

"At least, at least?"

"Is it really necessary?" I asked after hesitating briefly.

"Extremely necessary. How can I paint you properly if you won't take your clothes off in front of me? If I don't see your soul? I am a painter of the soul, not the routine exterior."

"Routine, routine."

"I think I could take off my tie," I said, falteringly.

"Wonderful! We'll try to make up for the rest with questions."

"Questions, questions!"

"Questions?" I repeated like the echo of an echo, barely stopping myself from saying it twice.

"Yes. I will ask you six questions so that I can discern some of your particulars. They are of a rather personal nature, but this cannot be helped. The questions would not be needed, of course, if you undressed, but since you don't want to . . ."

"Don't want, don't want . . ."

I started to loosen the knot on my tie. "Can this not be helped either?"

"What?"

"What, what?"

"This." I nodded towards the dwarf, although the painter was not looking in my direction, and even if he had it would have been hard to see anything through his blind man's glasses. "This repetition of your words."

"Does it bother you?"

"Bother, bother?"

"It grates on my nerves."

The painter laid his brush on the little shelf at the bottom of the easel, then cracked his knuckles. The dwarf immediately started turning the ball with his feet. He did it very skillfully. The ball spun quickly in place.

"He hasn't always been like that. Oh, no. If you'd only had the chance to hear him before. It was a real pleasure to listen to him. Such eloquence, such oratorical skill! It's hard to believe that now, wouldn't you say?"

"It isn't easy," I agreed.

"And the things he used to talk about! The quintessence of wisdom! Pure philosophy, indeed! For me it was the ultimate inspiration. He would talk so magnificently about the wooden dummy, and I transformed his words immediately into paintings. Into a whole cycle of paintings. My life's achievement. But I didn't finish it. I was just about to start my last canvas, in which the wooden dummy would finally be unveiled, when she appeared. And she showed her true face at once. She punished him without mercy. And do you know why?"

"No."

"Because of the ball!"

"Because of the ball?"

"Yes, because of the ball. This stupid, cheap, paltry ball!"

"Outrageous!"

"She wanted to take it away from him, but he, of course, couldn't give it to her. He was completely unable to think without it. She, of course, had no use for it. But since she couldn't get her hands on it, she took her revenge. You'll never guess what she did."

"I can't."

"She started to undress."

"I don't believe it!"

"Yes. The poor thing writhed and twisted, whined and groaned, but this didn't move her in the least. She continued heedlessly to the end. When she was finally in her birthday suit, he clearly couldn't bear it. He let out a terrible cry, then fell into this state. And she just laughed maliciously, put on her clothes and left. She didn't even take the ball, even though he could no longer prevent her from doing so."

"How cruel!"

"More than that. Brutal. But she'll pay for it. Even if I'm not able to complete the cycle about the wooden dummy, I can paint her. Completely nude, so everyone can see what her soul is really like."

"No one could hold that against you."

"I'll paint her for sure. But let's forget that right now. Are you ready for the six questions?"

I deliberated a bit. "I think I am."

"Very good. So, shall we begin?"

"All right."

"Do you like to trample on young wild strawberries?"

"No, I don't."

"I see. And have you ever dreamed of snails swimming upstream?"

"No, I haven't."

"Aha! Did you ever sneak snowballs into matinée shows at the cinema?"

"No."

"You didn't? And did you ever wonder how many stairs there are in the world?"

"No."

"Interesting. Did you ever want to be a spyglass, perhaps?"

"No, I didn't."

"Not even one single time?"

"Not a single time."

"As you like. Here is the last question. Did you ever make a phone call standing on one leg?"

"Never."

"Wonderful. You can put your tie back on. Your pose is over."

"And that's it?" I asked as I knotted my tie.

"Yes."

"You will paint me solely on the basis of those answers?"

"To someone who is perceptive they say a lot about you. Of course, it would be better if you'd agree to undress. Would you care to change your mind, perhaps?"

"No, I wouldn't."

"Fine, if there's nothing to be done, then we're finished. Please excuse me now. Soon there will be a tunnel, and I only paint when we're in one."

He cracked his knuckles. The ball stopped spinning at once. As supple as a spring, the dwarf jumped from his reclining position onto the floor. His feet touched the carpet runner the same moment the ball fell on his now empty seat. He bowed deeply to me and went to the door. First he put his ear against it, then after he heard something that I didn't, he knocked: three fast, two slow, three fast.

The response came from the other side without a moment's delay: three slow, two fast, three slow. The dwarf grinned from ear to ear, then opened the door theatrically and drew the curtain.

As I went out, I first heard "Good luck!" and right after it came the echo, "Good luck! Good luck!"

I turned to offer my own greetings, but the conductor closed the door before I had a chance.

He was now wearing a white coat over his uniform, with several chrome instruments poking out of the breast pocket. He pointed to the right of the door and said, "Please sit down."

A dentist's chair with its accompanying paraphernalia was there. I regarded it hesitantly.

"Just a routine checkup. You have no reason to worry. Make yourself comfortable, it will soon be over."

I sat down in the chair reluctantly. I squinted when he turned on the large round light, which brightly illuminated my head.

"Open your mouth, please."

After a brief hesitation I complied.

"A little bit wider, if you please. That's it."

He took a dental mirror out of his pocket, brought his face up close to mine, and started to inspect the inner surface of my jaw.

"He's a wonderful painter," he said. "If you'd only had a chance to see his cycle on the wooden dummy."

He grabbed me by the chin and pulled down a bit. My mouth was now yawning.

"But of course, that is no longer possible. He destroyed it. He told you, didn't he?"

I shook my head faintly, uttering a gurgling sound.

"He didn't? I see. I should have suspected as much. Then he must have told you that she is to blame for everything?"

I nodded my head, this time refraining from making any noise.

"Of course. The easiest thing is to point the finger elsewhere."

He returned the mirror to his pocket, then took out a dental probe and started using it on my lower left molars. I jumped when I suddenly felt pain.

"Everything is fine. The enamel is a bit worn, though. You should take more vitamins and eat fresh fruit, particularly pineapple and kiwi."

I tried to say something, but it was quite incomprehensible once again.

"As though the truth can be hidden. I'll tell you what really happened."

His brow suddenly wrinkled. He stepped back a bit.

"You've got a bit of tartar here. We'll remove it right away so it doesn't put pressure on your gums. Periodontal disease can quickly get the upper hand. You won't feel a thing."

In place of the probe he took up an instrument that resembled a miniature sword with a disproportionately long handle and started to scrape off the tartar.

"He had an argument with the dwarf, that's what happened. They have a strange kind of relationship, if you get my drift. But let's set that aside. In any case, after the argument the dwarf wouldn't tell him about the wooden dummy anymore. To spite him, the painter burned all his paintings. Down to the last one. He almost set the place on fire."

He took the sword out of my mouth. "Rinse, please." He indicated a ceramic glass half filled with water.

I closed my mouth with relief. It felt completely unhinged. I sipped a bit of water and sloshed it about, then spat into the drain on my left.

"When he saw the incinerated paintings, the dwarf fell into a stupor. He still hasn't recovered, and I'm not sure he ever will. She arrived when it was already all over. She tried to help. She gave the dwarf the ball and this revived him somewhat. And just see how the painter returns her favor. He spreads loathsome lies about her. Did he by any chance tell you that she took off her clothes?"

I verified this with a nod, not wanting to open my mouth just yet.

The conductor sighed deeply. "It's simply appalling how ungrateful people can be. And not just anyone, but artists! That's what is so devastating."

He put the instrument on the tray next to the chair, then handed me a napkin.

"You should go to the dentist more often," he said as I wiped my mouth. "Your teeth are in good shape, but at your age you need monthly checkups."

"Most certainly," I agreed.

"All right, we may now proceed." He waited for me to get up, then took off the white coat and threw it over the back of the chair. He rubbed his hands together and headed for the next door.

Since it wasn't closed, he just drew the curtain aside and motioned to me to go in.

When I entered the compartment, four tall girls sitting in the corner seats jumped to their feet. They were wearing camouflage uniforms and dark yellow helmets covered with netting, decorated with leafy twigs. The legs of their loose pants were rolled up to the middle of the calf, and their feet were in basins full of water.

"Salute!" rang out from the left-hand corner next to the window (whose curtain was drawn).

They raised their clenched fists sharply to the edge of their helmets in salute then quickly dropped their arms to their sides, remaining at attention. We all stood there without moving until I finally realized what was expected of me. I clenched my hand into a fist and saluted in the same way.

"At ease!" resounded from the same place.

The girls' stiff comportment relaxed only a little. They put their hands behind their backs and eased their stance as much as the space in the basins allowed.

"Please sit down!" came the throaty voice of the girl who had issued the orders. She indicated the seat next to her.

After I'd taken my place, the girls sat down too, backs as straight as boards. Their hands were placed on their thighs. They looked straight ahead, at each other.

Their stiffness was of short duration, however. It was interrupted by a new order. "Table!"

The girl to the right of the door got up at once, turned in her basin—without spilling any water—then took a small folding table from the luggage rack above her. She unfolded it skillfully and placed it in front of me, then sat down again. All this took no more than a few moments.

"Tablecloth!"

The girl across from the commander reached towards the storage space under the window and took out a folded orange tablecloth. She shook it open and spread it on the table in front of me. There was no need to adjust its position. Then she added an orange napkin.

"Utensils!"

The girl to my right put her hand under her seat and deftly pulled out a small suitcase. She lifted it effortlessly to her knees and opened it. It was full of various eating utensils. She took out a porcelain plate and put it on the tablecloth. Next came a knife and fork, and then she placed a crystal glass before me. Finally, she took a vase with fresh wild flowers out of a special compartment in the suitcase. This done, in a flash the suitcase was back under the seat.

There was no pause before the commander roared the next order.

"Food!"

Jumping up off her seat as though catapulted, the girl who had taken down the table said all in one breath:

"Infantry cheese in gunpowder eucalyptus sauce, three bayonet olives filled with almond shot, rocket liver commando style!"

"Beverage!"

The girl who had spread out the table cloth stood up and burst out:

"Tank red wine!"

"Recitation!"

Standing up quickly, the girl who had set the table said in a gentle, almost purring voice, "On a spring morning the ladybug alights on a dandelion."

All three sat down as one. Once again I needed a bit of time to figure out what I was supposed to do. I turned to my left and saluted again with a clenched fist. A brass gong and wooden hammer appeared out of somewhere in the commander's hands. The gong rang out.

As though he had been waiting outside the compartment, the conductor marched inside. He was carrying a large tray with a dome-shaped cover, and he had a large white napkin thrown over his arm. He stopped at the table and gave a brief bow. Then he bent over slightly and took hold of the handle on the top of the cover. Just as he was raising it we entered a tunnel.

This time the darkness was not complete. A bit of light came in from the corridor, under the three-quarters-closed curtain. Even so, I didn't see what was under the cover, because the conductor's bulky figure blocked most of the faint light.

He, however, didn't seem bothered by the darkness. He put the cover on the empty seat across from me and served my food with skillful movements. Then he filled my glass from a small wine bottle that was also on the tray.

I felt for the knife and fork. I had just managed to get hold of something soft on the plate, when the recitation began. I stopped the fork halfway to my mouth.

The poem was short. Some sort of haiku. The sun that has just risen illuminates a yellow flower. Enchanted, the ladybug settles down on it. The gentle breeze ripples the water of a nearby lake. The conductor spoke three verses with great élan and excitement, almost in ecstasy. Like a real actor. I lowered my fork after the first verse, so I was able to applaud heartily when it was over. I expected the girls to join in too. It might not have been according to protocol, but the poem, I thought, could not have failed to affect them. It must have touched even the most hardened military heart. Instead of applause, however, what followed was the exact opposite.

First there was a giggle, and then a guffaw. Soon the

whole compartment was echoing and probably the corridor too. I couldn't see the conductor's face in the dark, but it wasn't hard to imagine how he felt. I thought I heard his sobs through what were now waves of laughter as he removed the plate full of food in front of me and the glass full of wine. He put them on the tray and covered them. He turned on his heels, then marched sharply out of the compartment, accompanied by shrieking and mocking, unseemly exclamations.

When the curtain closed behind him, we came out of the tunnel. With the light back, silence reigned as though by unspoken order. The girls, who had been howling a moment before, were once again sitting like statues, hands on their thighs, faces serious, eyes gazing straight ahead.

"Clear!" The sharp order broke the silence.

It was all done in a trice, with *well-practiced* moves. One girl picked up the utensils and put them back in the suitcase, another took the tablecloth and napkin, folded them and put them in the storage space under the window, and the third folded the table and put it on the luggage rack, once again without spilling a drop of water from the basins.

They did not return to their seats after finishing their tasks. Once the table was removed, the commander stood up.

"Salute!"

Four fists sped to the helmets, then dropped to the side.

I didn't have to figure out what to do anymore. The reception was over. I got up but did not return their salute. It was against regulations, but I had to let them know what I thought of their outburst. I was boiling with anger.

I had just turned to leave the compartment when whistles echoed all around me. I couldn't imagine that women, even in uniform, could whistle so loudly. And then, as though this wasn't enough, when I reached the door, I was hit by a flurry of drops. There was no need to turn around to see where the water for this shower had come from. Striving to preserve my dignity, I passed through the curtain with head held high. The chorus of whistles went silent the same moment.

The conductor was waiting for me in the corridor. Instead of a tray and napkin he was now holding a tailor's measuring tape. He was wearing only his vest and out of its shallow pockets poked scissors, blue chalk and a small notepad with a pencil. Attached to the sleeve above his left wrist was a pincushion filled with pins.

He opened his arms wide. "What can I say? Outrageous impertinence! And simply because you didn't join them in poking fun at me."

"But why did they do that?"

"Ah, why. Because of the chocolate basin, that's why."

"Chocolate basin?"

"That's right. If you will allow me."

He put the end of the measuring tape by the knot of my tie. "Might I ask you to hold this here?"

I pressed on the semicircle of metal with my thumb. The conductor knelt in front of me and stretched out the tape. He took hold of it at the place where it touched the floor, then got up. He looked at the measured length, took the little notebook and pencil and made a brief note.

"The chocolate basin is the insignia of their regiment. It had been entrusted to their safekeeping. But they didn't look after it."

"They didn't?"

"No. Now let's see the width."

He went behind me and stretched the meter from one shoulder to the other, then wrote another number in the notebook.

"No one else is to blame. Did anyone force them to bet? No, of course not. But you know what military minds are like. They think that no one can beat them. Please be so kind as to stretch out your arm."

He measured from under my arm to the end of my sleeve. A third note went into the notebook.

"They were convinced they would easily win the bet. Could anyone outdo them in drinking wine? And a woman to boot? Not on your life! Allow me."

He opened up my jacket, then put the tape measure around my waist. He shook his head, looking at the number.

"You should pay better attention to your weight. It's much easier to put it on than take it off. Can you imagine how many bottles they drank?"

"I can't."

"Twenty-six! Believe it or not! Without eating anything. So much wine on an empty stomach!"

"Unbelievable!"

"I wouldn't have believed it if I hadn't served them myself. I tried to warn them that it would not end well, but all in vain. Who has ever brought unruly soldiers to their senses? They were disdainfully dismissive and simply ordered a new round. And afterwards, when they lost, they blamed me."

"You?"

"Yes, me. Allegedly I'd put something in the wine. As if that's possible. And what reason would I have to do that? Go on, you tell me."

"None."

"None, of course. But they had to find a scapegoat. Let's see your pant legs. Spread your legs a little, please."

I did as I was told. The conductor measured the inner leg, then wrote it down.

"There. Now we have all your measurements. In any case, if there had been something in the wine it would have affected her too. They drank out of the same bottle. But she remained fully conscious, while the girls finally passed out after the twenty-sixth bottle."

"*Who wouldn't?* That much wine would kill a lot of people."

"That's right. When they came to, instead of the chocolate basin they found their feet in tin basins. And that's not all. The bet says they can't take them out until they learn at least one haiku by heart."

"Only one?"

"Yes. But they won't, not for anything in the world. They would rather keep their feet in the basins indefinitely. For the sake of their pride."

"That sounds more like stubbornness to me."

"Exactly. You put your finger on it. Stubbornness, no doubt about it. And hypocritical stubbornness to boot. And do you know why?"

"No, I don't."

"Because they're pretending. Long ago they learned by heart that haiku about the ladybug and the dandelion, but they just won't admit it."

"Is that so?"

"Clear as day. They always request that I recite the same one. I've repeated it so many times that probably the seats in the compartment have memorized it, let alone four bright, perceptive girls. They don't take just anyone into the women's units. There is a strict selection process. After all, there are only three verses. But instead of repeating the haiku with me and freeing themselves from the humiliating act of keeping their feet in a basin, they would rather make vicious fun of me. So be it. It certainly isn't easy for me, but they are the ones who pay the price. What shade would you like?"

"Excuse me?"

"What shade of fabric? For your suit."

"Oh." I thought it over briefly. "White."

"An excellent choice. Many people wrongly consider that only a dark suit is appropriate for formal occasions, but that is a mistaken belief, of course. There is nothing more elegant than a white suit, particularly when the lighting is weak. You always stand out. What kind of lapels would you like, narrow or wide?"

This time I didn't hesitate. "Wide."

The conductor applauded. "Excellent. There is nothing as telling as a man's lapels. Narrow lapels are worn only by the narrow of mind, those with hidebound views, miserly and malign, and disposed to gout, while a man of the world is recognized above all by his wide lapels. Congratulations."

He stretched out his hand with the tape measure thrown over it and we shook hands firmly.

"All right, now let's move on." He headed towards the fifth compartment.

He opened the door without knocking and stuck his head through the curtain. I didn't hear him say anything. He soon pulled his head out and motioned me in with his hand. "If you please."

There were three passengers in the compartment. A young nurse in a white uniform was sitting on the left, next to the curtained window. Blond curls tumbled from under her white cap. There was a healthy, ripe look to her. Across from her sat an old man and woman holding hands, their heads drawn together. I'd never seen people as old as they were. They had completely wrinkled skin, inflamed eyes, very thin hair, and they were stooped. The frozen smiles on their faces looked like death masks.

As soon as the door closed, the nurse stood up and came over to me. Before I knew what was happening, she raised the bag she was holding way up high and sprinkled confetti all over my head. Then she clapped gaily.

"Happy birthday! Happy birthday!"

I stood there in bewilderment a few moments, sprinkled with multicolored paper flakes. "Whose birthday?"

"The gentleman's, of course," she said, indicating the old man.

"Oh," I replied, then bowed to him. "Happy birthday, sir."

The two old folks just kept on smiling. The nurse returned to her seat, swaying her hips. She pointed to the spot next to her. "Have a seat."

Before I sat down, I shook off a bit of the confetti. Only then did I notice that the carpet runner was practically covered with it.

"I'm sorry, I didn't know. Otherwise I would have brought a present, to be sure."

"It doesn't matter. The important thing is that you came. It means a lot to both of them." She looked at them tenderly.

"My pleasure." I bowed once again.

"How old do you think he is?"

I shrugged my shoulders. "Really, I wouldn't know."

"One hundred and seventy-six!"

"One hundred and seventy-six?" I said, aghast.

"That's right. Although you'd never say so. He looks at least thirty-five years younger, doesn't he?"

The nurse winked at me.

"Why, of course," I hastened to agree. "At least. Actually, I wouldn't think him more than one hundred twenty-eight and a half!"

"I thank you for the compliment in his name." The nurse smiled, and dimples appeared at the corners of her mouth. "If you're interested, I'll tell you what he has to thank for his longevity."

"Of course I'm interested," I said without a moment's hesitation.

"The time he spent in prison."

"In prison?"

"Yes. He spent exactly one hundred and six years, eight months, eleven days and two hours in prison. He was sentenced to life in prison, but was recently released for good behavior."

"If I'm not being unduly inquisitive, why was he sentenced to such a long punishment?"

"He ate his first wife."

I swallowed the lump in my throat. "Ate?"

"That's right. Not all at once, of course. Over seventy-six days. This was taken as a mitigating circumstance during the trial, otherwise he might have been sent to the gallows. But please don't ask me anything else about that ghastly event. Talking about it always upsets him and that's not good for his weak heart. In any case, he has completely repaid his debt to society."

I looked at the old man across from me. It seemed that nothing could cloud the cheerful serenity on his face.

"Madam is his second wife, I presume?"

"Yes. They met seventy-two years ago by pigeon carrier mail. She was only eighteen at the time. They exchanged photographs and it was love at first sight. They married in prison not long after."

"Wasn't she bothered by what had put him in prison?" I asked in a low voice.

"Not at all. Love works wonders. She closed her eyes to it. You can imagine how happy she was when she finally saw him free. But this romance wouldn't have had a happy turn if he hadn't become friends with the cook in prison."

"The cook?"

"Yes. He was also in prison, sentenced for the brutal murder of his seven daughters, although he never confessed to the crime. As a young medical corps lieutenant, the cook spent several years as a prisoner of war in the jungle. He barely survived, but he brought an amazing talisman back with him. A glass corkscrew. He received it from a tribal chieftain whose son he'd saved from certain death from a tropical insect bite."

The nurse reached into her pocket and took out a bag of candy. "Help yourself," she said, holding it out towards me.

"No, thank you, I don't eat candy."

"Please, it's his birthday, you must help yourself to something."

I took one, but just held it in my hand without unwrapping it.

"The glass corkscrew gives longevity to its owner. The cook, however, decided to kill himself, unable to bear the burden of being unjustly sentenced. Before he poisoned himself, he gave the talisman to the only friend he had in prison."

"Why, that's just like in an old fairy tale."

"Yes, except this one won't have a happy ending."

"It won't?"

"No, he doesn't have the talisman anymore. He certainly won't live to see his next birthday."

"You don't say. And what happened to the glass corkscrew?"

"He gave it away."

"Whom did he give it to?"

The nurse drew a bit closer to me and whispered. "You already know who he gave it to. It's not hard to guess."

"You mean . . ."

She gave a brief nod. "As soon as she entered our compartment, he took the talisman out of the leather bag he wore at his waist and gave it to her. As though he'd just been waiting for her to appear."

"But why?"

"So that he could die with his wife. Her days are numbered. The doctors don't give her more than three and a half months. They will end their lives together. They have made a vow to die together. Isn't that romantic?"

"Yes, it is."

"A genuine melodrama."

"Truly."

The nurse got up. "Now we must say goodbye. There's a tunnel coming up, and these two don't like to miss any of them. Who can blame them after all the decades of separation and deprivation? They don't have many opportunities left to be intimate."

I got up as well. "Will you stay inside too?" I asked, taken aback.

"Of course. I'm a nurse. They might need my help.

At their age such things don't go very smoothly. And my presence won't bother them in the dark."

I bowed towards the snuggling couple. "Goodbye."

"Goodbye," replied the nurse. "They greatly appreciate the fact that you visited them on this of all days. They will never forget you." The dimples appeared at the edges of her mouth again.

I put the piece of candy in my pocket and went out into the corridor. The conductor was standing in front of the door.

"This way, please." He motioned towards a four-sided canvas screen to my left that looked like a changing booth in a clothes store. It was shoulder high.

I went in between the two sides that were ajar, and he closed them after me. Although it didn't look like it from the outside, there was quite a bit of space within. A white suit was hanging on one wall. A white shirt was draped over it, and on the floor were white shoes and socks.

"You can hand me your clothes over the top, and leave your slippers inside. I'll take care of everything."

I started to undress. "Is this really necessary?"

"Yes, it is. You must be properly dressed."

"What for?"

"For the last compartment, of course."

"Oh, I see." I handed my coat to the conductor.

"Did she mention the cook?"

"Yes."

"That part of the story has the most holes in it."

"Really?"

"Above all, it's not at all certain that he was a prisoner of war, and even less in the jungle."

"You don't say."

"Various rumors about that are making the rounds. The most convincing one to me is the story that he was a missionary to a cannibal desert tribe. And an unsuccessful missionary to boot. Instead of him converting them, they converted him."

"Are you saying . . . ?" I handed my shirt and tie over the screen.

"Yes. And I'll tell you one more thing, but in strict confidence. It's quite possible that there was no cook."

"What do you mean?" I asked, taking off my socks and slippers.

"It's quite simple. The missionary was actually the gentleman himself. He returned to civilization with the talisman of longevity, which is all right, but with cannibalistic habits, which certainly is not. Judge for yourself. If that weren't true, why would he have eaten his wife? Whoever would do something like that out of the blue?"

"No one, I suppose."

"There, you see. I'm telling you, there's something fishy there. Without even mentioning the nurse. With her things become dark and shady."

"What are you saying? I never would have thought . . . She seemed so good-natured and harmless. She even offered me candy." I threw my pants over the top of the screen.

The conductor's face suddenly turned pale. "You didn't eat any, did you?"

"No, I don't like candy. I put it in my jacket pocket."

"Thank heavens! I forgot to warn you. I'll get rid of it at once. You can't even imagine what might have happened to you!"

"What?" I took the shirt off the hanger and started to put it on.

"You're better off not knowing. The best thing is to have nothing to do with cannibals."

"The problem is that they want to have something to do with you."

"That's true, unfortunately. I hope the suit looks good on you."

"I'm sure it will." I took the pants. "The cloth looks first class."

"The best that could be found. It doesn't stain at all, as you will see. In addition, it needs almost no ironing. And it is very soft."

"The pants aren't tight around my waist. That's very important. I can't stand tight pants."

"If the measurements are taken properly, the suit should fit like a glove. Many tailors don't take sufficient care and then wonder where they went wrong."

I put on the jacket. "It looks perfect."

"Just wait until you see yourself in a mirror."

I looked over the top of the screen. The conductor was holding a large mirror in front of him.

"Just a moment." I bent down and quickly put on the shoes. They were of very high quality white leather, light and supple. I pushed the side of the screen and came out.

"Wonderful," exclaimed the conductor, eyeing me from head to toe. "Here, see for yourself."

In the mirror I saw an elegant man dressed to the nines, who would fit quite nicely into any formal occasion. "Excellent," I concurred.

"Just two more details," said the conductor. He held out a white hat from behind the mirror and then leaned the large oval between two windows in the corridor.

The hat also seemed made to order for me. I nodded my head in satisfaction.

"And here's the bow tie."

It was over his left sleeve, large and white, as was to be expected.

"Allow me." He raised my shirt collar, attached the tie in the back then lowered the collar. He stepped back a bit and examined me once again.

"There. Now everything is perfect. You are utterly ready."

He led me towards the last compartment. "She only receives when we're in a tunnel," he said, once we had stopped in front of the door.

"But then it's dark."

"Right. In addition, I will have to put a blindfold over your eyes." He took a long band made of white silk out of his right pocket.

"Why is that?"

He tied the band behind my head, underneath the hat. "Because that's the way things are done. It's not too tight, is it?"

"No."

"Can you see anything?"

"No."

"Good. We'll soon be in a tunnel. Be ready. When I give you a push, go inside. Stop right by the door. You will have to stand, unfortunately, because all the places are taken. You won't find that too difficult, will you?"

"No."

There was a brief moment of silence and then the conductor spoke again. His voice was low and pleading.

"If she asks about me . . . although she won't, of course . . . why should she, anyway . . . who am I, after all . . . but nonetheless . . . a man mustn't lose hope . . . what would life be without hope . . . so, if she mentions me . . . please tell her that I am here . . . always . . . all she has to do is . . . regardless of everything . . . nothing else is important except . . . she is still . . . tell that to her, I implore you. . . ."

That very moment he nudged me in the back. I hesitated a bit because I didn't hear the door opening in front of me, but I took a step forward all the same. I stopped after the second step.

"Take off the blindfold." A woman's voice came from my left, somewhat farther away. It was soft and lilting.

I untied the knot at the back of my head. When the blindfold fell off, I wasn't in total darkness as I'd expected. The shapes on the five seats were outlined by a weak glow, as if edged by tiny sparks. They were disproportionately large, occupying the same space that passengers would have.

The wax button to my right was hexagonal, with a double ring of holes that flickered with a bluish tinge. The horned egg in the middle had two bent protuberances in its lower part resembling stunted limbs, with points that seemed to glow. The wooden dummy next to the window had been pierced at the top, and out of the hole flowed drops of liquid fire. The chocolate basin to my left contained something gelatinous and fluorescent. The glass corkscrew on the seat next to it was periodically suffused with short green flashes that seemed to come from somewhere inside. The last seat in the row was the opaque heart of darkness.

"Put the blindfold back on," said the darkness.

I did as I was told.

"What do you see?"

"I don't see anything."

"Take a better look."

I took a better look. "I see an apple that has fallen off a tree."

"What is it like?"

"Large, green and juicy."

"Put it back on the tree."

"Put it back?"

"Yes. Apples should be on trees, shouldn't they?"

I held it up to a branch and it clung to it as though drawn by a magnet.

"Doesn't it look nice there?"

"Lovely."

"And now look again."

"I see the figure of a black queen."

"What is her hair like?"

"Long and red. Wavy."

"Stroke it."

I shook my head. "I don't dare."

"Don't hold back. She will enjoy it."

I gently drew my hand over the cascades. The queen lit up with joy and ran forward.

"What a light step she has."

"As though she's not even touching the ground."

"Look once again."

"I see a large purple ball."

"Throw it up into the air."

"Into the air?"

"Yes. Don't worry, nothing will happen to it."

I threw it up. The ball started changing color as it got smaller and smaller. The purple turned to turquoise, the turquoise to blue, the blue to white, the white turned colorless.

"Did it disappear?"

"No, it's still going up. You have set it free. What do you see now?"

"I see a yellow flower."

"What is on the yellow flower?"

"A ladybug."

"Blow on it softly."

"But I'll frighten it."

"No, you won't. Ladybugs love air currents."

I blew a little puff towards the ladybug. As though set in motion by a breeze rippling the water of a lake, it spread its wings and fluttered off.

"Isn't it gracious?"

"Like a ballerina."

"Look one last time."

"I see the bars on a prison door."

"Pull them apart."

"How can I pull steel bars apart?"

"It's not at all hard. Try."

I flexed my muscles, but no effort was needed. The bars gave way as though made of rubber and stayed apart.

"That is your way out."

"My way out?"

"Yes. Go through the opening."

"Now?"

"Now. Everything has been done."

I had already started to pull myself through when I remembered something. I turned towards the heart of darkness.

"What about the conductor?"

"Tell him not to lose hope. That's what is most important."

"That will make him very happy," I said, beaming.

"I know," replied the melodic voice.

On the other side of the bars I was still in darkness. Then I felt someone's hand on the back of my head, and the white silk blindfold fell off my eyes. Squinting, I saw before me the space at the end of the carriage. To the left was the door leading to the back platform and to the right was the clothes closet.

"If you please," said the conductor, stepping in front

of me. In his left hand was a medium-sized brown leather suitcase. "Everything is neatly packed inside. The laundry has been washed, the suit ironed, the shoes polished, the hat brushed, and the coat dry-cleaned. There was a stain in the lining that wouldn't come out any other way."

"I am extremely grateful. How much do I owe you for all you've done for me? This wonderful suit, too, and I must finally pay for the ticket."

"Think nothing of it! Any payment is out of the question. It was an honor to be of service."

I held out my hand. "Thank you once again from the bottom of my heart."

We shook hands, but he held onto mine.

"Did she say anything, perhaps?" he said in a small voice.

"Oh, it almost slipped my mind. Yes, she said not to lose hope, that's what is most important."

The conductor suddenly fell to his knees before me. He brought my hand to his lips and kissed it. I tried to pull it away, but he wouldn't let go. He pressed his cheek against it.

"I knew it . . . as soon as I saw you . . . your kindness . . . it was all so clear to me . . . no one else . . . would she otherwise . . . just how much . . ."

His voice faded into sobbing. I felt my hand turn wet, and stopped trying to pull it free.

The conductor stayed in that position a little longer, and then seemed to come out of his daze. He abruptly let go of my hand, got up and wiped the tears off his face with his fingertips.

"Please excuse me. A moment of weakness. It will not be repeated. You surely understand, I hope?"

I nodded. "Certainly."

"Good. Now, unfortunately the time has come to say goodbye. It always comes, there's nothing to be done. Such is the life of a conductor. Meetings and farewells. I believe that in spite of everything you had a nice time with us."

"I had a very nice time."

He handed me the suitcase, then unlocked the door and motioned towards the platform. I went out onto it and he followed behind.

We stood there facing each other for several moments. It seemed as if one of us might say something else, but when this didn't happen I smiled, bowed, and descended to the station platform.

2. The Teashop

Miss Greta was delighted to see a teashop across the street from the entrance to the railway station. The train she'd arrived on had been a quarter of an hour late, but the train she was meant to take for the rest of her trip had left on time. The next possible train wouldn't leave for around two-and-a-half hours. She could have spent that time reading in the waiting room, but that didn't seem very appealing. She'd never liked waiting rooms, and then what would she have to read on the train? About eighty pages were left in her book, just enough to shorten the last part of the journey. It would certainly be much nicer in the teashop. And in any case it was time for her afternoon tea.

She stood at the main entrance to the station for a few moments, uncertain about what to do with her suitcase. Although it was heavy, she had only to cross a small square to reach the teashop. Even so, there was no reason to lug it along, particularly since the drizzling rain was now getting harder. She turned this way and that until she found a sign that directed her to the left luggage window. The short, oldish man behind the counter had an extremely red nose, typical of people inclined to tipple, but he didn't smell of alcohol. He lifted the bulky suitcase effortlessly with one hand and gave her a baggage check.

Miss Greta opened a large umbrella with alternating triangles in two shades of brown that matched her coat, shoes and handbag. She waited for two cars to pass so they wouldn't spray her and then headed across the square with swift little steps. Even though she chose carefully where to step, it was inevitable that she got splashed. When she reached the arched roof covering the entrance to the teashop, she turned around and shook out her umbrella, returning a flurry of drops to the rain.

Standing in the doorway, she looked around the long room. The waiter at the counter on the right, a heavyset man in his early forties with bushy sideburns and a pencil-thin *mustache*, was wearing a white short-sleeved shirt and a green vest. The slender cashier with bright red hair and oversized glasses, writing something down at the cash register, was also dressed lightly, in a white blouse and the same green vest.

There weren't many customers. The elderly man sitting in the corner to the left of the door was reading a newspaper. He raised his eyes briefly when Miss Greta entered, then went back to his reading. A young couple was sitting next to the large window. They were leaning over the table towards each other, their noses almost touching, talking in low voices. At the back of the room was a woman in a navy blue suit wearing a hat of the same color. Her elbows were on the edge of the table and her head was resting in her hands as she looked at the steaming cup in front of her, lost in thought.

Miss Greta headed for an empty table away from the window. She didn't like to expose herself to the gaze of passers-by. She took off her coat, hung it on the coat rack, and put her umbrella in the brass stand underneath it. When she sat in one of the heavy armchairs covered in green plush, she seemed to be sucked into it.

She didn't have to open the long, thin menu with a cover of the same green. In the afternoon she always drank chamomile tea. Suddenly, though, she decided to make an exception. The circumstances were unusual and there were so few deviations from daily routine in her life. She shouldn't have been there at all, but since chance had brought her to the teashop, why not make good use of it? An impish desire filled her to do something reckless in a place where no one knew her. She would order the tea that seemed the most unusual.

The menu had four densely-filled pages. She'd never heard of most of the teas and had tried only a few, even though she'd been drinking this hot beverage in the morning and afternoon regularly since childhood. Reading through the splendid selection, she wondered with a tinge of sorrow why she limited herself to the humdrum. This had once seemed a virtue, but now she could not remember why. She shouldn't be inhibited, at least as far as tea was concerned. Now was the chance to make up a little for what she'd missed, albeit belatedly.

Along with the names of the teas was a description of their beneficial effects. Some astonished her, others brought a smile to her lips, and yet others made her blush slightly. She didn't even know there was tea made of cabbage (a "salutary digestive"), spinach ("relieves the pain of spondylosis") and carrots ("helps fight anemia"). Nettle tea was thought to improve one's memory and moss tea purportedly calmed tense nerves, while papyrus tea rekindled the flames of desire.

The fourth page offered teas that were preposterous.

Had circumstances been otherwise, the level-headedness that made Miss Greta proud would have forced her to frown at what she read. Just now, however, it did not seem to be tasteless frivolity. What difference did it make if they were preposterous when they sounded so nice? She could have asked what the teas were really made of, but decided not to because that would only dispel the magic.

Tea made of wind chased away apathy, tea made of clouds brought a yearning to fly, moonshine tea inspired lightheartedness, spring tea made you feel young again, tea made of night led to sinful thoughts, tea made of silence filled you with tranquility, tea made of mist brought great joy, snow tea offered hope. She could have chosen any one of these teas. The best thing would actually be a mixture of them all. She was deficient in everything they promised.

But in the end she didn't order any of them. She chose the last one on the menu—tea made of stories. This was partially influenced by the brief recommendation next to it: "You need this". The decisive element, however, was that she adored stories. She read them every day, as ritualistically as she drank tea. Whenever she was in low spirits, she would scold herself for living a better and fuller life in the world of stories than in the real world, but this dismal conclusion never dissuaded her from reading, and as soon as she got caught up in a story her depression disappeared the same moment. Since she was already determined to try the most unusual tea, this was the right choice.

She closed the menu and put it on the table. That was a signal for the waiter to approach.

"Good day," he said with a smile. "May I take your order?"

"Good day," she replied with a fleeting smile. "Tea made of stories, please."

She didn't say it very loud, overcome by an embarrassment she would not have felt had she asked for an ordinary tea. Even so, in the silence of the teashop her soft words seemed to reach everyone's ears. The cashier stopped writing and turned towards her table. The man next to the entrance looked at her over the top of his newspaper. The young couple with eyes only for each other turned their heads in unison towards her. Even the lady in the navy blue suit stopped staring at the cup on the table and looked at her with interest.

Miss Greta blushed and lowered her head. She felt like she'd been caught committing a crime. She alone was to blame for this predicament. Had she ordered chamomile tea, as she should have, no one would have batted an eyelid. It served her right for having no self-control. Tea made of stories, indeed. What must they think of her?

She was rescued from this discomfort by the waiter. He bowed, his smile broadening.

"Of course, ma'am. Right away."

She didn't raise her head when the waiter left to make her tea. She stared for some time at the folded hands in her lap, almost physically feeling the inquisitive and scornful looks. But when she finally mustered the courage to glance quickly around the teashop, she noted with relief that the others had ceased to be interested in her. They had all returned to what they'd been doing before.

Several minutes later the waiter put before her a white cup in the shape of an inverted bell, its handle resembling a mouse's ear. The tea was the same green color as the vests of the teashop staff. She smiled at the waiter, thanking him with a nod of the head.

Instead of leaving, he stood there next to her table. Embarrassment filled her once again. She didn't know why he was still there or how she should react. In the end she concluded that the best thing would be to act as though he was nowhere near her. She would start to drink the tea. That was why she'd ordered it, right? What else could she do, in any case?

She brought the cup to her lips and blew a little on the steaming green liquid. She tasted it cautiously, anxious about the heat and the unknown taste. The tea was mild with a suggestion of bitterness. She had the feeling she'd tasted it before, but was unable to identify it. It seemed to be a mixture of almonds, dogwood and something else that escaped her. She put the cup back on the saucer.

"Is it to your liking?" asked the waiter.

"Yes," she replied after a moment's hesitation. "Very much."

"That's nice. So, now we can move on to the stories." He indicated one of the two empty armchairs. "May I?"

She watched in bewilderment as he sat down without waiting for her permission.

"The stories?" she repeated after he had settled in his chair.

"Yes. The stories that go with this tea. You took the tea made of stories, didn't you?"

She wanted to say she hadn't imagined it would be like that, but then it would look like she hadn't known what she was ordering and this would only compound her distress. She had no idea what was to follow, but there was no turning back. Just see what the desire to do something reckless had brought her.

"Of course," she agreed.

The waiter coughed slightly, like an actor clearing his throat before going onstage, and then began.

"Up until the thirty-third execution, the executioner had successfully performed his duty. He belonged to a respected family of executioners that had been doing this responsible job impeccably for six generations. There had never been any complaints about their work; they had even been decorated for their exceptional devotion and diligence during periods of great social upheaval. Families of the convicted would write sometimes and thank them for the skill with which they'd *dispatched* their loved ones from this world with the least possible suffering.

"A veil of secrecy surrounded the reason why the youngest scion of this honorable family tree suddenly decided to break with their glorious tradition. He refused to offer any explanation, thus his reasons could only be surmised. The last execution he'd performed was thought to have influenced his choice, although he couldn't have been particularly affected by the elimination of a baby-faced hardened criminal who had mercilessly killed eleven librarians, first forcing them to put on firefighting uniforms and read the same excerpt from an ancient epic, while he accompanied them on the harp, wearing diving equipment.

"It was also conjectured that the fact that he'd recently joined an association to protect white bear cubs had influenced his decision to leave his profession. This had allegedly dulled the insensitivity that is a characteristic of every good executioner, but that wasn't very convincing either. It is a well-known fact that compassion for animals usually does not go hand in hand with compassion for humans. Haven't most of those who've left the bloodiest trails behind them been remembered for their touching gentleness towards some cat, dog, horse, parrot or crocodile?

"Be that as it may, the executioner withdrew to a tuberculosis sanatorium in the mountains even though he was perfectly healthy. That is when he started to collect rare mountain flora. The head nurse supported him in his efforts, as she herself was an amateur botanist. Sometimes, when she was not on duty, she would take long walks with him across the slopes and peaks and they would return with a multitude of new specimens for their herbariums.

"Rumors about a sentimental attachment between them inevitably spread through the sanatorium, but they paid no attention, offering no grounds for this gossip in their public behavior. Nothing can be said for sure, of course, as to whether or not anything happened when they were out of the doctors' and patients' sight. If it did, it was very discreet, as befits such a highly dignified institution. Everything might have been disclosed in the end if it weren't for an unfortunate incident that thwarted the would-be lovers.

"When one of the patients, a retired mining professor, found out that in spite of everything there was no hope and he had only a few weeks left to live, he became gravely concerned about the fate of the large hoard of napkins that he'd been collecting since he was a schoolboy. Since he had no heir, he had no one to leave it to. He wrote to various museums, offering his collection free of charge, even including his considerable savings to maintain it. For the most part there were no replies, and those he did receive hurt him with their indifference and often unconcealed disdain.

"In the throes of a nervous breakdown, without considering the consequences, the professor put all his napkins in the middle of his room and set them on fire. The fire blazed into a fury and quickly spread to the neighboring rooms, then engulfed the whole floor and finally the entire sanatorium, an old building without proper fire precautions. In the chaos that ensued, all efforts were focused on saving the helpless patients, so what the executioner did passed almost unnoticed.

"When it was already too late to stop him, he was seen rushing into the flaming building. By some miracle he made his way to his room on the first floor and threw a bunch of herbarium folios through the closed window. In spite of everyone's exhortations to jump and save himself even at the risk of injury, he went back for the rest of the herbarium folios, although tongues of fire were already flickering all around him.

"Nothing else came flying out the window and he did not appear at it again. The sanatorium burned to the ground. The remains of eight bodies were found in the charred ruins. This, however, did not agree with the number who had disappeared, which was nine. After great effort, when they identified the burned bodies, it turned out that the only one to disappear without a trace was the executioner. It was concluded that his body had been vaporized in the fire, and he was officially declared dead."

Finishing the story, the waiter bowed briefly. Miss Greta was tempted to applaud, but held back, returning his bow with a smile. This was the kind of story she liked best—romantic and mysterious. True, there had been too much violence in it for her taste, the hero shouldn't have been an executioner exactly, and many people had died in the fire, but she shouldn't grumble. After all, it was only a story.

She was no longer sorry she'd ordered this tea. What

a wonderfully clever idea it was to offer a good story along with an equally good drink. The only pity was that it had been so short. She wondered what would happen if she ordered another one. Did the waiter have a new story for every new cup of tea? First she had to finish the one in front of her as it would be inconsiderate not to do so, even though it had most likely cooled off while she was listening to the story. She lifted the cup and took a long sip, surprised to find that it was still quite hot.

"Wonderful," said the waiter when the cup was on the saucer once again. "So now we may continue."

Without giving an explanation, he got up and headed back to the counter. Along the way he passed the cashier, who was headed for her table. Without even asking for permission, the tall woman sat right down in the same armchair as the waiter. She took a green handkerchief from the breast pocket of her vest, removed her oversized glasses and started to wipe them. This made her chestnut brown eyes look smaller. When she put her glasses back on she didn't start the story right away. She gazed at Miss Greta for several moments, as though looking through her.

"After the calamity in the sanatorium, the head nurse decided to change her profession. Not even the avalanche of attractive offers she received after winning recognition for saving the patients from the fire could dissuade her from this decision. She withdrew from the world for several weeks and when she came back she was like a different person. Everything about her had changed: the raven-haired woman had become a blond, her classically-cut dark dresses were replaced by striking leather suits in bright colors, and instead of being modest and gentle she was sharp and gruff.

"But the biggest surprise was her choice of new profession. She became a stuntwoman, showing an acrobatic agility and courage that were unimaginable even to those who knew her best. She was undaunted by the most perilous assignments and soon the best film directors started to ask for her. A brilliant career awaited her, but then something happened that made her cut it short.

"The assignment was to shoot down a dangerous waterfall with two other stuntpeople in a rubber boat. All protective measures were taken and the scene had been gone over in detail, but the security cable snapped during filming. Instead of being held back, the boat and its occupants ended up on the rocks at the bottom of the waterfall. By some miracle, the former nurse was the only one to survive, suffering just minor scratches.

"The investigation that was conducted established that it had not been an accident as first thought. The cable hadn't snapped, it had been cut. Who had done it remained a mystery, although the two people who died turned out to have a motive. They were actually part of a strange love triangle. He was obsessively in love with the new stuntwoman, even though she rejected his advances unrelentingly, while she was jealous of her, convinced that she'd stolen the man she loved so desperately.

"Once again the nurse turned stuntwoman withdrew for a long time and came back drastically changed. Her blond hair was now red, light sportswear replaced the leather suits, and her behavior changed accordingly—she was cheerful and coquettish. The change in profession was also a surprise. She joined a traveling circus.

"First she tried a number of secondary jobs. She took care of the books, looked after the trained animals and was makeup artist for the clowns. She might not have advanced if it weren't for two young illusionists who came to the circus and needed an assistant. They said they were brother and sister, although their behavior was suspicious from the outset. They were demonstratively tender with each other and often held hands, so rumors started to circulate that they were lovers who had a reason to lay low or, worse yet, that they were having an incestuous affair. But since their act soon became the hit of the show, no one made an issue out of it.

"All of their acts were brilliant, but the one in which the former nurse took part won the greatest acclamation. A glass box resembling a sarcophagus filled with water was placed in the middle of the circus ring. The assistant, dressed in a turquoise one-piece swimsuit, would take a deep breath and plunge into the water. The box was closed and locked with huge padlocks and then the two illusionists threw a turquoise cloth over it. The suspenseful moments that followed were accompanied by appropriate tension-inducing music. When the audience was already fidgeting fretfully, the cloth was removed, revealing the empty sarcophagus with the padlocks still in place. That same moment there would be a fanfare of trumpets, the curtain would open and the assistant would run into the ring, completely dry, to the audience's thunderous ovation.

"Unfortunately, after the seventeenth performance this act, along with all the others put on by the young illusionists, was removed from the program. Something inexplicable happened that made them leave the circus. After their departure it was said that just before the strange event relations between the brother and sister had suddenly cooled. They stopped holding hands and were overheard quarrelling in low voices. It was even said that tears were seen in the brother's eyes. These stories, however, were not to be trusted.

"One thing set the seventeenth performance apart from the previous ones. When the fanfare sounded, no one appeared from behind the curtain. Everyone except the illusionists was surprised. They alone remained unruffled, as though everything was perfectly fine. There was another fanfare, but again no one ran out before the audience. The failure might not have been so complete if news about the act hadn't spread, with the result that the audience knew what to expect. The mysterious disappearance of the assistant from the sarcophagus was certainly striking in itself, but her absence at the end caused first a commotion and then a great chorus of whistles. It almost closed the entire show.

"After the show was over, everyone set out in search of the former stuntwoman, but in vain. She had disappeared as though the earth had swallowed her up. The brother and sister were questioned but claimed to know nothing of her fate. They denied having anything to do with the unpleasant event, indicating that the assistant might have been dissatisfied with her secondary role and this had led her to leave.

"The ringmaster briefly thought of notifying the police, but in the end he didn't because this would merely have saddled him with greater worries. His ears were still filled with the whistling; if the police were to start sniffing around the circus his audience would disappear entirely. In any case, no offence or crime had been committed that would require police intervention. Everyone had the right to leave the circus whenever they felt like it. In the end the two illusionists were forced to abandon the troupe. The circus lost a highly popular act, but this was the price that had to be paid."

The cashier bowed at the end just as the waiter had. This time Miss Greta had to clap, although she did it almost soundlessly, barely putting her palms together. The story seemed tailor-made for her—full of romantic suggestions and secrets, without too much violence. True, two of the main characters had died in the stunt episode, but this seemed unavoidable. If it was any consolation, love had guided them to their deaths. Love was also in the background of the circus event. She was curious to find out more about the relationship between the brother and sister, and of course what had happened to their assistant.

She thought of asking the cashier, who remained at the table after the end of the story. There certainly must be a continuation, particularly since the first two stories were connected. And then she remembered that she hadn't had to ask for anything the last time. If she was not mistaken, it had been enough to take a sip of tea to get a new story. Perhaps it might work again. It wouldn't hurt to try. And she had to finish the tea anyway.

Swallowing a new sip, she wondered who would talk this time. Probably the waiter. The easiest thing would be to take turns until the customer drank all the tea. After all, they weren't professional actors accustomed to giving long performances, although they certainly were deserving of praise. They were very skilled at storytelling, letting the listener enter easily into the spirit of the tale. They must have acquired this skill through frequent repetitions. Tea made of stories was undoubtedly a favorite in this teashop.

But when the cashier bowed once again and headed back towards the cash register, Miss Greta had a surprise in store. She watched in bewilderment as the young couple sitting at the table by the window approached her instead of the waiter. Smiling, they sat in the two armchairs without saying a word. There was no time to think about this unusual turn of events because the young man started the story right away.

"After they left the circus, the two illusionists split up. He found work as a cook on a luxury ocean liner. During one of the cruises through tropical seas he met the rich young widow of a notorious arms merchant who had died when a stray golf ball hit him clean in the temple. For some time the tabloids played up the story, claiming it hadn't exactly been an accident, but if there were any conspiracy it was soon covered up.

"The cook attracted the widow's attention with an excellent soup composed of mushrooms, figs and snails that he made from an ancient recipe that was said to have a strong aphrodisiac effect. She asked to meet him, and when he was brought before her he captivated her at first glance. She continued to see him under various pretexts, always leaving large tips, even when there was no reason.

"Her attempts to lure him into her cabin, however, met with failure for a long time. The ship's crew was strictly forbidden from any sort of fraternizing with the passengers, and entering their cabins was considered a particularly serious offence. Nonetheless, on the penultimate evening of the cruise the widow's intentions finally succeeded thanks to her cunning and to alcohol that the young cook was unaccustomed to drinking.

"No one knows for sure what happened that night in the cabin. When the maid entered in the morning she found him sound asleep on the floor, while the widow lay dead in the bed. The ship's doctor established that she had died of a heart attack, so he could not be blamed for her death. Even so, he lost his job on the spot and disembarked at the next port."

At this point, the young man turned towards the girl and nodded. She nodded in return and took up the story.

"After leaving the circus, the sister illusionist found work as a restorer in a museum. She soon caught the eye of the director, who had a bad reputation as a womanizer. Behind him were four broken marriages and seven daughters, as well as numerous adventures, but this did not stop him from new entanglements, even though he was no longer a spring chicken.

"The restorer coldly rejected his advances, but this only made the director more resolute. In the end, when it was clear that he would fail, he resorted to the last means available, something that had yet to let him down. He accused the restorer of doing an unprofessional job and threatened to fire her unless she satisfied his desires.

"She protested, informing him that she had just made a discovery that would not only prove her professionalism but also make her famous. Working on a late Renaissance canvas, she came to the realization that it was some sort of palimpsest. Underneath it was a considerably older work by a famous master from the end of the Middle Ages that had been considered lost forever. She invited the director to be the first one to see this painting under a painting.

"Not suspecting anything, the director rushed to see it, already devising plans on how to take credit for the discovery. But what he saw turned him numb. The original painting portrayed a scene from hell. A monstrous devil was taking great relish in torturing a sinner who had spent his life in vicious debauchery. When he looked at the sinner's face more closely, it was like looking into a mirror. By some miracle the old master had depicted his face to perfection.

"At that moment something seemed to break inside the director. Instead of firing the innocent restorer, he resigned immediately and soon retired to a remote monastery where he lived in extreme abstinence from all physical pleasure, outshining many of the ascetics in this regard. As a sign of recognition, the restorer was offered his position, but she refused without an explanation and left the museum too."

The young girl and boy nodded to each other once again, then he took up the relay.

"The former ship's cook soon got into trouble in the port. He was sitting by himself at a table in a disreputable tavern when a bunch of noisy, drunken sailors burst in. They started to pester the guests, pouncing in particular on the pretty, young and timid tavern maid. They heckled and pinched her aggressively, and when one of them, who was exceedingly arrogant, grabbed the girl by the hand and pulled her onto his lap, trying to kiss her by force, the former illusionist could no longer sit there indifferently. He jumped up to protect the poor girl.

"Everything happened in a twinkling. Blows were exchanged, jugs and chairs went flying, knives flashed. When the skirmish was over, the arrogant sailor was twitching on the floor in the throes of death, his stomach skewered, while everyone else had fled. The terrified girl begged her savior, who had an oozing wound on his upper arm, to escape as well, even offering to hide him in her room upstairs, but he refused and waited for the police to arrive.

"Although the girl and all those who witnessed the tavern brawl testified in his defense at the trial, he was still found guilty of murder and sentenced to twelve-and-a-half years of hard labor. In prison he was put in a cell with an older convict who was soon to be released after being locked up almost a quarter of a century. A crime of passion had put him there. He'd found his wife in bed with his best friend and in a moment of blind rage killed them both with one single shot from a crossbow.

"The old man turned out to be very well-read. Since the young convict was also proud of his erudition, the two of them began spending long hours in stimulating conversation, amazing each other with their knowledge and sagacity. When the day of his departure was quite near, the old man decided to tell his last cellmate, in whom he had infinite trust, something that he had not confided to anyone.

"In the prison library, which was surprisingly well-stocked and contained some truly rare editions, he had come across a book that mentioned a secret society with a strange belief. All creatures capable of thinking were nothing more than cells in the gigantic brain of a cosmos that was striving to grasp its own meaning. The former cook found this very interesting and wanted to read the book without delay. But this, unfortunately, was not possible. The old man told him that the book had disappeared from the library after he'd returned it and all trace of it had been removed even from the card catalogue.

"Luckily, however, the old convict had a photographic memory, so he was able to pass on faithfully everything he'd read, including the part about the complex and dangerous rite of linking with the cosmic mind. Wonderful possibilities opened up for those who survived it, for they would acquire almost divine abilities. The old man admitted, a bit reluctantly, that he had started the ritual once but stopped at the last moment, lacking courage. He asked his cellmate whether he might have the necessary bravery, and he agreed without a moment's hesitation.

"The next morning when the guards came to release the old man, they found him sitting in the corner of his bed, terrified, shaking his head, mumbling something unintelligible. There was a wild look in his eyes and his hands trembled uncontrollably. There was no trace of the other convict. It was impossible to learn what had happened in the cell during the night. The old man never emerged from his stupor, so instead of finally finding himself free he was locked up again, this time in a mental asylum for the poor."

Finishing the story, the young man bowed towards Miss Greta, but there was no time for her to return the bow because the young woman started right away.

"Leaving the museum, the former illusionist and restorer joined an expedition into the jungle, where the ruins of a temple from a previously unknown ancient civilization had been found. The team was led by a famous archeology professor, a tall and learned man with graying hair that only made him more attractive. She fell in love with him immediately, but had to hide her feelings because the professor's wife was present. She was also a prominent scientist and still lovely, although no longer in her prime.

"On the other hand, suspecting none of this, the professor's two assistants had their eye on the former restorer. They competed for her favor, even though she made it perfectly clear that their efforts were in vain.

Who knows where their rivalry might have led—a duel with machetes was only avoided by a hair—if it weren't for a discovery that pushed their aching hearts into the background. Underneath the temple they found a network of underground passages filled with priceless treasure. In addition, unknown hieroglyphics covered the walls.

"They all threw themselves enthusiastically into their work, but not for long. The three male members of the team soon came down with a mysterious disease that brought shivering, high fever, exhaustion and vomiting. Something in the stale air of the passages seemed to affect only the men. The expedition had to be suspended so the ailing men could be taken urgently to the hospital.

"Although the professor tried to dissuade the two ladies, mentioning in his delirium an ancient curse, they decided to take their last chance and go down below the temple one more time before the helicopter arrived. Just as they reached the passage, everything around them started to tremble and give way. It looked like a strong earthquake, but it turned out later that the trembling had not been natural. They rushed for the way out, but only the professor's wife was saved.

"When she had recovered a little from her shock, she confided to the professor alone what had happened in her last moments underground. Both of them could have been saved, but just when they reached the stairs there was a powerful flash of light in the chaos behind them. She was blinded an instant; when she regained her sight she saw the young woman going back down again. She screamed at her to come back, the passages were liable to collapse at any moment, but she paid no attention. She continued, arms stretched out in front of her as though spellbound. There was no time to try to rescue her because that's when the granite walls around her started to crack as though made of plaster. She was barely able to make it to the surface."

Just as the young man had done before her, the girl bowed after she had finished. This time Miss Greta applauded without the slightest hesitation, unconcerned that she was disrupting the silence in the teashop. She had to express her delight and in return received one more bow in unison from the two young people. The other stories had been wonderful, but these surpassed them. Particularly the girl's—so full of passion, tension, mystery. She didn't like the episode in the prison very much in the boy's story. It had been interesting, but she was bothered by the absence of female characters, although she knew it would be hard to have them in a men's prison. The episode in the tavern, though, had been perfect in all respects.

Not only were the stories superlative, they had also been told with such inspiration. These two could not be just customers in the teashop, as she'd mistakenly assumed. They were most certainly professional actors. Only actors were capable of presenting events so skillfully and convincingly, as though it had all happened to them, each one picking up where the other left off. She felt like clapping again when she realized this. It was beyond all expectations: keeping two actors on standby just so one of the customers would be able to order tea made of stories.

And then a thought made her stiffen. She hadn't paid attention to the price of the tea she'd ordered. She hadn't thought it necessary. Tea didn't cost very much. But there was no way that this one could be inexpensive. Perhaps the waiter's and cashier's stories had been free, but actors had to be paid. Who would perform and hang around wasting time between performances without remuneration?

Unable to control her impatience, she opened the menu again with a mixture of dread and embarrassment, even though she was not alone at the table. She hoped that the two actors sitting there smiling at her would not figure out what she was doing. Her eyes flitted down the fourth page. What she saw brought relief along with confusion. The only place where the price was not listed was for tea made of stories.

She closed the menu and in her bewilderment, almost unconsciously, just to occupy her hands, raised the cup and took one more long drink that emptied it. The color seemed to have turned a darker green and it was now tepid, but strangely enough this did not lessen the flavor. On the contrary, it seemed to have acquired an additional quality. As she lowered the cup, the young couple stood up, bowed one last time and returned to their table by the window.

Miss Greta wasn't sure whether the performance that went with the tea made of stories was over or not. It seemed to her somehow unfinished. Perhaps the waiter or cashier would return to the stage, or both of them together. It wouldn't be surprising. What did happen, though, was the last thing she expected. A new couple headed towards her table: the woman in the navy blue suit and the man who had been reading a newspaper.

He bowed, she smiled, and then they settled into the armchairs. There was no introduction. The woman started her story at once.

"The archeologist's wife left him soon after he recovered from his fever. The illness seemed to have changed him. He blamed her without letup for what had happened when she'd gone underground for the last time. He seemed to regret the loss of his assistant more than the disappearance of an ancient civilization's shrine. She felt doubly betrayed: as a wife and an expert.

"She gave up archeology and joined a charitable organization that sent its members to different parts of the world, where they helped the unfortunate. Her first assignment took her to a desert region hit by starvation and contagious disease. There she met a handsome missionary who helped her get accustomed to the terrible conditions. Working selflessly with him day in and day out, she started to feel an attraction for him, although he could almost have been her son.

"She would have kept this secret to herself, of course, if the young missionary had not contracted the disease. Its course was unremitting: it led first to blindness and then death. Conscious of the fact that there was nothing to be done, he refused to go to hospital, wanting to stay in the mission until the end. She never left his side, particularly after he lost his sight. When his end drew near, she finally confessed her love for him.

"He, however, refused to believe her, claiming that she only felt compassion because of his condition. Overcome by despair, she thought of catching the disease herself in order to prove her love, but failed in this intention because death was faster. The missionary died in her arms, unconvinced of her love, and she, totally crushed, decided to return home."

There was no pause. As soon as the woman in the navy blue suit finished, the man adroitly picked up the thread.

"The old man spent three and a half months in a mental asylum for the poor. He finally recovered, although it was impossible to get anything out of him about what had happened that fatal night in the cell. A free man at last, he found work as a cemetery guard in a small town in the provinces. He soon caught sight of a young woman who came every Monday morning right after eleven when there were usually no other visitors.

"Dressed in elegant mourning and always wearing sunglasses, she would go to the spot where a retired ornithologist had lain in rest for more than eighty-five years. She would spread out a gray blanket on the grave, sit on it and then take a chess set out of her bag. She would line up the pieces, always putting the white ones in front of her, and the match would begin. After she made her move, she would look towards the tombstone and then, as if receiving instructions, play a black chess piece. Sometimes the games were drawn out. Once it was almost five before she left the cemetery.

"The old man was a devoted chess player himself, so it was no wonder that he was compelled by the unusual rivalry. In the beginning he kept his distance, watching surreptitiously, but since his eyesight was already poor, he gradually came closer, though fearing that the woman in mourning might chastise him for disturbing her. But there was no word of reproach, not even when he approached quite close and stood right behind her back.

"He was rather surprised to learn that this was not amateur chess, as he'd expected for some reason. These were sophisticated matches between players of equal stature. They always ended in a draw, which was reached after a great battle. Each time before she left, the woman would take a queen's chess piece made of marzipan out of her bag and put it on the tombstone. The birds would devour it by morning.

"Several months passed before the cemetery guard

mustered the courage to ask the woman in mourning if she would play a game of chess with him. He was convinced she would refuse, but she agreed without a moment's hesitation. Without a word, she indicated that he was to sit on the blanket across from her. Three hours and forty-two minutes later he got up from there the loser. Even worse than the defeat was the fact that he was certain he hadn't made any mistakes.

"Then, for the first time, the woman took off her sunglasses and spoke. She told him that if he wanted to live he should never play chess again, he should quit his job at the cemetery and leave town. He hesitated not a moment as to whether to do as she said. He went straight to the cemetery office and resigned, then went to his rented apartment, packed his few belongings, and headed towards the train station. He bought a ticket to the farthest destination that could be reached by the next train."

"All that remained was for her to take a train on the last part of her arduous trip from the desert regions and the dismal memories that tied her to them. She was alone in the compartment for a long time, and then she acquired a traveling companion at the station in a small town with a pretty cemetery next to the track, full of tall cypress trees.

"She was pleased to see that the elderly man kept to himself. He greeted her politely, sat next to the window and gazed out pensively. She certainly would not have liked to engage in small talk. She went back to reading the archeological journal that she'd bought at the airport."

"Two stations later another passenger entered the compartment. He was on the brink of middle age, heavyset, with bushy sideburns and a thin mustache.

He bowed and sat down next to the door without a word. Silence reigned in the compartment until they stopped unexpectedly in a tunnel. An announcement came over the P.A. system that there had been a rock-slide nearby and the rails would be cleared in about fifteen minutes. No one got up to turn on the light nor did anyone suggest it."

"When the train came out of the tunnel, only the passenger who was last to arrive was sitting in the compartment. He was in the same place, staring straight ahead. The darkness had hidden what had happened to the other two passengers. There was no trace of them, not even their luggage."

"The passenger got out at a large station where several lines intersected. Just as he stepped onto the platform, out of the blue he made the most important decision of his life. He would no longer be an executioner. He would interrupt the family tradition of the past six generations. And he would not tell anyone why. It was none of their concern, after all."

"As he left the train station he almost ran into a woman who suddenly started to turn this way and that, looking for the left luggage window. Although she hadn't noticed him, he mumbled something in apology and then continued on his way."

The stories were over, but Miss Greta did not clap. She sat there without moving, watching the woman in the navy blue suit and the older gentleman stand up, nod briefly and return to their seats. When they sat down, she lowered her eyes to the empty cup in front of her.

She stayed like that, staring for some time, as though seeing something on the bottom that other eyes could not discern. She finally turned towards the coat rack, reached into her coat pocket and took out the baggage check she'd received at the left luggage window. She turned it over several times and then raised it a little as though wanting to show it to everyone. Then she tore it up. She was delighted to receive the resounding applause that greeted her after she placed the pieces of paper on the saucer next to the cup.

3. The Square

I

It was always crowded in the Square Café on Saturday, even without such pleasant weather as this, so unseasonably warm for early spring. Just before noon it seemed that the whole town had flocked to the large square with the fountain in the middle. The faces of the strollers were like sunflowers, raised towards the sun that had been so stingy during the long winter.

Only two waiters had been needed the previous Saturday to serve the customers who filled all the seats inside, getting out of the rain that had been pouring without letup for weeks. Today eight tables had been placed in front of the café, so backup had to be called in.

If the bad weather hadn't changed, Vesna wouldn't have been expected at work until Monday. Probably she alone was dejected by the window filled with blueness that morning. She knew that the telephone would soon start to ring and, of course, she wouldn't be able to say no. The extra shift would be handsomely paid, but she would gladly have turned down the additional money to be able to spend the weekend reading, as she'd intended.

She briefly toyed with the idea of venting her anger on the customers, refusing to pay them professional courtesy. But they weren't to blame for the predicament she was in, and in any case she didn't look good wearing a frown.

Soon enough she realized that things could be worse. If she'd been assigned to work inside, there'd be three tables less to cover, but in conditions identical to those in winter. This way, she had her hands full, but at least she was in the sun. The cheerfulness that soon brightened her face as she skillfully worked the tables was not just professional. The beauty of the day—like all other beauty—had an intoxicating effect on her.

The museum on the square was almost empty. On a cloudy Saturday it would have been full of visitors, but today people clearly favored natural beauty to that made by human hands. Andrei also would have preferred to be outside, but he had to wait patiently until three o'clock when the museum closed. Then another twenty or so minutes would pass until he finished all his guard duties at the end of the shift. Nevertheless, he hoped that a little bit of sun would still be left before the early twilight.

The museum had no windows so that external light did not mix with the internal lighting. When there was no one in the four ground-floor rooms he supervised, Andrei would go into the central atrium. The quadrangular space rose up through the entire height of the building like a huge light well. It ended above the fourth floor with a frosted glass roof. The diffused sunlight that poured down from there seemed somehow deficient, but it was more appealing than the cold artificial light in the rooms.

Whenever he went back among the paintings, he felt a certain disaffection. Particularly when he was alone there. People came from far away to admire the works of art, but long ago they'd ceased to have any effect on him. That was the main drawback of being a museum guard. When you are surrounded by the same beauty every day, at some point you stop noticing it. He felt this to be a punishment that was all the harder to bear since he didn't know what he'd done to deserve it.

Friday was the only day Nada didn't clean the movie theater right after the last show. That day there was a late show at midnight after the regular shows at six, eight and ten o'clock. There was no reason to wait until two in the morning to do what could be done on Saturday before the first show. As a rule, there were hardly any viewers at the late show, so there wasn't much to clean anyway.

After tidying the theater quickly at the end of the ten o'clock show, Nada would take her place at the ticket window. She stayed there until the beginning of the midnight show, then rushed to catch the last bus for the suburbs where she lived. The movie theater was small, with only twenty-eight seats, and it was rare for them all to be filled. Owing to the theater's modest revenues, she had to cover two jobs—cleaner and cashier. The only other employee was the movie operator who also tore off the ticket stubs at the entrance.

The Rex Theater's repertoire was behind the poor attendance. It didn't put on films that attracted a big audience but those that some of her friends derisively called artsy. Over time, Nada had started to take this mocking tone as a personal affront.

Before she started working at the Rex, she hadn't

been much of a filmgoer. Now, instead of being bored in the foyer while the movie was playing, she preferred to spend time in the auditorium. It hadn't taken long for her to become an art film buff. She watched every movie as many times as it was shown. Although she might have had a hard time explaining why she liked art films so much, if someone were to ask, she would simply say that they were beautiful.

This was enough of an explanation for her, just as it was enough to say that this Saturday was beautiful. If it had been raining, as it had the past days and weeks, she wouldn't have gone to work until five-thirty. Today she was already there at two. She would clean the auditorium and then take the chair from the ticket booth out in front of the theater. She would sit there and enjoy herself, watching the busy square until sunset, which coincided with the first show.

Of all the people on the square, Zoran was the only one who could hold his head towards the sun and look straight at it. He was not afraid of injuring his eyes. Once sight has been lost it cannot be further harmed by staring at the fiery ball.

He never wore dark glasses or carried a white cane, refusing these tokens of blindness because he hadn't come to terms with his handicap. Indeed, he'd been told by doctors long ago that there was no chance of regaining his sight, but that only concerned his eyes; during the years of darkness he'd discovered that it is possible to see with the other senses.

He saw best through his ears. When he listened to music, he clearly heard colors. Each instrument had its own. The sound of the violin was dark red, the cello was purple, the viola resembled saffron, the contrabass was orange, the harp ocher, the piano was a sort of lemon, the guitar was chestnut, the flute violet, the bassoon was azure, the French horn aquamarine, the trumpet was reseda, the trombone dark green, the timpani were silver, the dulcimer was ash and the drum almost black.

His favorite was the sky-blue color created by the oboe. He'd learned to play this instrument so he could hear it whenever he wanted. Over time he'd grown skillful and even ventured to play in public. He would play for about twenty minutes on the square around noon almost every day.

If the weather was bad, he would play under the arched roof of the passage in front of the second-hand bookstore, whose owner looked kindly upon his concert. When it was a nice day, such as this Saturday, he went out into the sun, but not near the center of the square where the gurgling fountain drowned out the oboe.

At the bottom of the open instrument case that he placed on the ground in front of him was a piece of cardboard with the inscription I PLAY FOR FREE in large letters. Even so, whenever he finished he would find not only bills, but a variety of objects inside, mostly books or trifles bought in the second-hand bookstore.

He didn't sense any bad intentions behind these gifts. Those who gave them knew that he couldn't read or see the shapes, but he could listen as someone read to him, and long ago his sense of touch had become much more acute than that of those who had the use of their eyes.

II

Although Vesna had a good memory, she could not remember who had been the last person to sit at table number four. This was not unusual given the great turnover that day. Customers didn't stay long at the eight tables in front of the Square Café. They had a quick drink and then joined the river of people out for a stroll. Their places were immediately taken by others. Sunny days encouraged movement, unlike rainy days when the customers would stay a long time, as though anchored there.

New customers were standing next to table number four, waiting for her to clear it. She rushed over and picked up the bottles, cups, glasses, spoons and napkins. Then she put the bill and money from the previous customers on her tray, replaced the pink paper tablecloth, and motioned with a smile for the three young girls and a boy to sit down.

When one of the girls pulled out her chair, she found a large notebook with a brown binding on it. She picked it up and looked at the waitress quizzically. Vesna took it and her smile broadened, as though in apology.

This happened every day. The café customers were proverbially forgetful. They usually left umbrellas, hats, keys, eyeglass cases and books, but also stranger things. The proprietor of the café had a showcase where he kept unusual objects that had never been claimed by their owners. It contained, among other things, a worn-out pair of false teeth, a quiver for arrows, a medal with a ribbon, a switchblade, a pack of condoms, a turtle shell, a gaudy wig and even a cracked glass eye.

Vesna took the notebook into the café and gave it to

the cashier behind the bar. No explanation was needed. The woman took it without a word and leaned it against the side of the cash register. That was the usual place for forgotten items. It would stay there for the next two or three days. If no one came looking for it, the proprietor would decide whether it was worth putting into his collection.

If Vesna could remember who'd been sitting at table number four, she might see the person again. Most of the guests were regular customers at the Square Café. More than once, thanks to her alone, a forgotten item had been returned to its owner who hadn't even come looking for it, since he hadn't the slightest idea that he'd left it there.

Now it all depended on the forgetful customer. If he or she didn't appear very soon, and the proprietor decided that the notebook didn't suit him, it would end up in the garbage.

Just before closing, Andrei made his final round of the rooms. This was not necessary because the last visitors had already left his part of the museum more than half an hour ago, but he was a conscientious guard who followed the rules.

He found the large brown leather drawing portfolio in the fourth room. It was lying on the middle of three benches, blending in mimicry of the color of the wood. He'd seen such portfolios before, brought by art students who came to the museum to practice, learning from the great masters. They would spend hours studying them in detail and drawing. But this was the first time anyone had ever left their portfolio behind.

He stared pensively at the embossed leather surface. As far as he could remember, no one had come with a drawing portfolio that day. But evidently his memory was unreliable. His attention was proportionate to the number of visitors. Besides, his thoughts had also been preoccupied with the beautiful day, so it was no wonder he'd missed this. Indeed, it could have lain there a long time without attracting his attention.

He wondered what to do with it. The rules said that all found items were to be reported to the security service. But that meant writing a report, which would take at least fifteen minutes, thereby reducing the already short time he had left to spend in the sun.

Andrei was a conscientious guard but also a practical man. He would spare himself the trouble if he simply didn't report the portfolio. There would be no harm since its owner couldn't get hold of it until Monday when the museum opened again. He would put it in his locker and discreetly return it to the room on Monday morning.

When its owner turned up, what would be more natural than to contact him first? And if he or she didn't appear, Andrei would make the report at the end of that working day. He wouldn't be in a hurry then. The forecast was for protracted rain starting again tomorrow.

Nada always followed the same order when she cleaned the movie theater. Starting from the last of the seven rows, she first vacuumed the four seats covered in burgundy plush and then the matching carpet. The moviegoers took those seats first, while those closer to the screen were usually empty. She didn't even have to clean there, but did it just the same. There would always be a bit of dust, and she thought it a sacrilege to show art films in a dusty auditorium.

There wasn't much to clean in the back rows either.

The people who came here were different from the public in other movie theaters. They didn't leave scattered popcorn, empty plastic cups, chewing gum stuck under the seat or even more unseemly things. Actually, there was usually nothing but puddles on the floor left by their umbrellas. There was enough space in the foyer for a cloakroom where coats and umbrellas could be left, but there was not enough income to pay someone to work there.

The puddles from the previous night's late show had long since dried. When she finished vacuuming the seventh and sixth rows, Nada was tempted to stop cleaning and go out into the sun. Even if there was some dust in the other rows, this would not spoil the first showing very much, and she would certainly vacuum the whole auditorium before the second show.

Knowing that this would give her a guilty conscience as she sat in front of the theater, she decided on a compromise. She would quickly vacuum just the carpet and not the seats. After all, they hadn't even been used. She hurried to the fifth row.

A surprise was waiting for her in the first row. There was something on the raised seat of number four. Because of the poor lighting she didn't recognize it until she got up close. It was a CD in a brown see-through plastic box. She picked it up carefully as though it wasn't a commonplace item and turned it over, searching for something more specific, but found nothing. There wasn't any sleeve and nothing was written on the disk except that it was a DVD and not a CD.

What surprised Nada was not so much the object as where she'd found it. Why would someone sit on the worst seat in the theater? That seat was taken only on rare occasions when the auditorium was full, and the late show the night before had certainly not been one of them. Only five tickets had been sold for the ten o'clock show also.

She mused a while over this unusual event and then shrugged her shoulders. It was stupid to stand there in the gloom racking her brains while everything was shining brightly outside. It actually made no difference how the DVD got there. Someone had left it, and if they wanted it they would come looking for it.

She returned to the foyer, placed the plastic box on the counter in the ticket booth, put the vacuum cleaner in the corner, picked up the chair and went out into the sun.

Someone always listened to Zoran's concerts even when the weather was bad, and today quite a lot of people had gathered. He was not aware of the size of his public until their applause echoed from all sides once he had finished. He always felt awkward as he bowed to people he couldn't see. He hoped that they would be no less enthusiastic even without his handicap.

He stood there for a while after the applause died down. When he could tell by the sounds that the circle around him had broken up and he was no longer the center of attention, he knelt down by the case. Before he could put the oboe inside he had to take out what had been put there in spite of the warning.

First he felt for money. He knew inevitably it would be there. He sighed and shook his head after he'd collected quite a sum. He put the bills in the breast pocket of his shirt. When he got home, he would put today's earnings with the rest that he kept in a shoebox. He didn't have any plans for the money. He put it in a box simply because he had to keep it somewhere.

The same box held the letters that a secret admirer regularly left on Saturday. The long envelope was there again today. She admired his playing in grandiose terms and considered him to be a kindred spirit to whom she could confide her most intimate feelings. She was convinced the two of them would make a perfect couple and that she alone would understand him perfectly. At the end of every letter she promised to approach him the next Saturday, but this had never happened, and the new letter never mentioned the promise that she'd made.

The case was full of objects too. He had no difficulty recognizing them by their feel. There were two books, a small picture in a frame, a brass figurine of three monkeys holding their hands over their eyes, ears and mouth, a large wooden block with two holes on one side, a long-necked vase, an enormous comb that could only be used for decoration, and a round bottle that probably contained some fragrance.

He was delighted when he felt the last item, a CD. He hadn't received music as a present in a long time. Strangely enough, his listeners rarely thought of rewarding him with something that really had meaning for him. He would keep only this out of all the gifts. It was the only one that seemed fitting. Like some sort of exchange. He had received in return what he himself had given.

He would take the other items to the second-hand bookstore. The owner would take them with feigned hesitation and excessive gratitude. It was a tacit agreement between them. The second-hand bookstore owner's kindness towards Zoran's playing in front of his store came at a price.

III

Monday mornings were never very crowded in the Square Café, and today only three tables were taken. If the weather had been nicer there might have been more customers, but the rain that had started on Sunday morning was still pouring without letup. The square's Saturday radiance now seemed a distant memory. Swollen, leaden clouds had descended almost to the roofs of the tallest buildings on the square. They'd had to turn on the lights in the café just as if it was already growing dark.

This gloomy atmosphere would have been easier for Vesna to take if she had had more work. After serving the four customers, she busied herself behind the counter for a while, doing superfluous tasks just to pass the time. Then there seemed to be no point, so she leaned her elbows on the counter, nestled her face in the palms of her hands and stared blankly out the café window at the wet grayness of the empty square.

If her boss found her in that position he wouldn't criticize her in the least. He wasn't bothered by idleness if the customers were taken care of. But he would get angry if he saw her with a book in hand. She would have loved to spend these free moments reading, just to take her mind off the terrible weather. But she could do nothing because of her boss's extreme intolerance. Vesna suspected it was because he didn't read at all. When she finally found another job, she would have to make a biting comment to him about it before she left.

She stared out the window for about ten minutes, then sighed and looked around the café. Nothing around her moved. The two old regular customers were completely immersed in their broadsheet newspapers, and the young couple was almost touching noses over the table above half-emptied glasses with straws, completely preoccupied with each other. The cashier's head was bowed, as though looking at something in her lap, but Vesna knew that she was dozing.

Her eyes rested on the notebook still leaning against the cash register. No one had asked for it yet. She doubted her boss would decide to keep it. It wasn't quirky enough for his taste. He would probably throw it away that very day. She hesitated for a moment, then went up to the cash register silently and took it, careful not to disturb the cashier's slumber.

If her boss were to appear suddenly, he couldn't hold anything against her. Even he had to know that a notebook wasn't the same as a book. The only person who had the right to chide her was its owner, but she greatly doubted that he or she would turn up. Her conscience pricked her just slightly when she opened it and started to read.

Andrei rarely went into the atrium on rainy days. The diffused light seemed hazier than usual then, almost like mist, and the monotonous drumming of the rain on the glass roof only heightened the dreariness. He didn't like the cold neon lightning in the rooms either, but it seemed the lesser of two evils.

There were no visitors yet. This was not unusual for a Monday morning, particularly on such a day. Very bad weather kept people away from the museum the same as very nice weather. No one might even appear until noon, when the students would start to drop in.

He wandered through the enormous rooms, feeling their emptiness press against him. If he'd been in another part of the museum where everything wasn't so familiar, he would at least be able to admire the beauty of the exhibited works, not like here where he hardly even noticed it anymore. The museum administration liked to keep the guards in the same part of the museum for the very reason that they knew all its details perfectly and were not distracted by beauty that would lessen their vigilance.

He sat on the broad middle bench without a back in the fourth room and stared at a large landscape. Six-and-a-half years ago when the museum had hired him and all of this had been new, his favorite place had been in front of this painting. The brightness it radiated seemed to burn his eyes. The gently waving field of poppies seemed ablaze under the yellow sphere whose heat was almost palpable.

After seeing it every day, his fascination had inevitably started to wane, until the painting finally became the same as the others whose magic had worn off. Now he tried to revive his former passion, hoping the radiance of the ripe summer it depicted might lessen the dejection that had engulfed him as soon as he'd walked into the rain that morning. But his hopes were in vain. The landscape no longer radiated a thing.

He lowered his eyes from the painting to the bench and stared for several moments at the leather portfolio next to him, unaware that he was even looking at it. He'd taken it from his locker and returned it there as soon as he'd arrived, certain that someone would come in search of it as soon as the museum opened. But more than an hour and a half had passed since then and no one had appeared.

He picked it up and ran his fingers briefly over the uneven brown surface. He knew he had no right to see what was inside. No painter, not even a beginner, likes anyone to look at a work in progress. If it weren't for his dejected mood, he most likely would have resisted the temptation.

Trying to justify himself, he reasoned that there would be no one to witness his offence. He leaned a little to the side and glanced through the door into the third room. This was unnecessary because, in the muffled silence of the museum, his skilled ear would have heard any visitor as soon as they entered the first room from the atrium. But as an unskilled offender he had to make doubly sure.

Then cautiously, as though someone really was watching, he opened the portfolio.

NADA REACHED THE MOVIE theater quite a bit earlier than planned. She'd taken care of some administrative work that had piled up the week before. She'd been convinced that she would spend a lot of time standing in line, but the crowds in front of the various payment windows were much smaller than she'd expected. The awful weather seemed to have discouraged people from the usual Monday crush.

She was relieved to have shortened the time spent in those places since she hated standing in line and dealing with paperwork. Now that she'd finished earlier than expected, she was in a quandary. If she'd waited in line as long as she'd feared, she would have reached the theater at three-thirty and spent the slightly more than two hours until the first show doing the weekly in-depth cleaning of the auditorium.

Now she had enough time to go back home, but the thought of the almost one-hour bus ride to the suburbs and back again was not very appealing. What would she do then, just hang around her apartment for a while? She didn't know what she'd do in the movie theater that early either, but she'd find something to while away the time. Anything was better than staring out a bus window at a cheerless view distorted by streaks of pouring rain.

After she'd thoroughly cleaned the auditorium and vacuumed the screen as well, she returned to the foyer. She sat in the ticket booth and stared blankly through the glass doors. If she had known how to operate the projector, she could have given herself a private showing of the day's movie. The fact that she would watch it three more times didn't bother her. One can never get enough of beauty.

But even if she had known how to mount the film, she would have thought twice before doing so. The movie operator was a considerate and obliging man, as cat owners often are, and he had four of them. But he didn't like anyone to meddle in the projection room. He wouldn't even let her clean in there; he did it himself.

And then it occurred to her how to pass at least part of the time until six. The DVD was still on the counter in front of her. No one had come for it the day before. If the owner showed up, it wouldn't be until right before the first show. And besides, the theater was still closed.

Just to be on the safe side, she went up to the doors and locked them. Then she took the brown case and headed for the wall facing the ticket booth where there was a black metal bracket with a small television and a player, one below the other. Sometimes they received movie trailers and played them before the show.

She turned on the television, put the DVD in the player and took the remote control into the booth.

She had no idea what it contained, but just now she thought that anything was better than staring at the rain as she would have on the bus. In any case, if she didn't like it, she could always turn it off.

She pushed the "play" button.

LIKE MOST STORES ON the square that were open on Sunday, the second-hand bookstore was closed the next day. Zoran didn't go out then because for some reason he felt he didn't have the right to be there without the bookstore owner. Most likely the man wouldn't hold it against him, but all the same. In addition, even when the weather was good he couldn't count on a large public on Monday, and in such a downpour he'd be lucky to attract even one of the rare passers-by.

Nevertheless, he asked to be taken to the covered passage at his usual time. He didn't feel like sitting at home. He'd tried to play for himself, but even though the drapes were drawn in the room, all the oboe produced were the colors of the heavy clouds crushing the world. There wasn't even a trace of the clear sky's deep blue.

He hoped that playing in this place, even without an audience, would clear up the weather at least a little. He took out the oboe, leaned the case against the wall so it wouldn't touch the wet sidewalk, and started a composition that had always summoned the most delicate shades of blue. But he stopped right after the prelude.

Surrounding noises had never bothered him very much before, but now no matter how hard he tried to ignore the drumming of heavy drops, it interfered hopelessly with his music. It didn't even help when he lowered his eyelids in an unconscious attempt to close himself off even further from the outside world. He simply could not block out the jagged sound that sullied everything generated by his instrument.

If only there were some way to get rid of it. Being outside, he couldn't just listen to music and eliminate the rain. Or could he? He remembered the Discman he always carried with him for those occasions when he wanted to listen to colors and was unable to play himself. The flat device was in his jacket pocket along with the small earphones that could now be his salvation.

He reached to take it out, but his hand stopped in mid-air. The Discman would be of no use. When he'd left home he hadn't properly prepared for this irregular outing. He didn't have a single CD with him. If the second-hand bookstore or a nearby music store were open he could borrow or buy one. Everything on this colorless day seemed to conspire against him.

He reached for his mobile phone to call for them to pick him up since he had nothing left to do there. Just before he touched the left button in the second row from the top, something suddenly crossed his mind. He closed the phone that hung on a cord around his neck, picked up the oboe case, opened it and slipped his hand into the small pocket under the lid. His lips spread into a smile.

He'd completely forgotten the CD he'd been given on Saturday and tucked away there. It made no difference what music it contained. Anything would do to chase away the rain. With swift movements he put on the earphones, opened the Discman, put in the CD and started it.

IV

Vesna closed the notebook on the counter in front of her, then raised her eyes to the café windows. She was not surprised at what she saw. The square was bathed in radiance as though the sun itself were pouring over the stone flags. The puddles had all disappeared, as though it hadn't been pouring a moment before.

Andrei closed the portfolio and placed it on the bench. He stood up and headed for the door out of the fourth room. His pace quickened in the third room, he started running in the second and he sped through the first. When he burst into the atrium he found a blinding beam of light pouring down from above. The frosted glass roof posed no obstacle whatsoever.

Nada pressed the "stop" button on the remote control but the screen did not go blank. On the contrary, it was glistening, showing a familiar sight. She smiled and then turned her head towards the glass doors so she could look directly at what was on the television. The brightly-lit square was even prettier that way.

Zoran took off the earphones. He could hear colors even without the music. They were all around him, red-hot and blazing. He swayed, stunned by their force. He seemed to be in the center of a soundless crescendo. And then the colors started to take shapes that became increasingly visible.

Vesna took off her apron, came out from behind the counter and headed for the door. The four customers were sitting stock-still, as though on a photograph. She stood in front of the café for a moment, head raised, as her face hungrily absorbed the sun's warmth. Then she headed across the square towards the fountain.

Andrei continued running down the long hall that led out of the museum. He was aware that dashing about like that was inappropriate in such a place, but this meant nothing anymore. The call of the sun overpowered all other considerations. He was already halfway to the fountain when he realized that he could slow down. He was no longer in a rush to go anywhere.

Nada looked once more at the frozen picture on the screen, then left the booth. Before she went out, she looked through the glass doors at the square for several moments. No more streaks of water distorted the world. But it was not until she went outside and headed for the fountain that its full magnificence swept over her.

Zoran walked out from under the covered passage. He no longer had to do it circumspectly, feeling the sidewalk in front of him with his foot. The fiery forms around him had stabilized. He could even see them with his eyes closed, but felt it was more decorous to keep them open. None of the others making their way towards the fountain had their eyes closed.

Vesna sat on the wide stone parapet on the southern side of the fountain and looked in amazement at the section of the square in front of her. What had once been buildings was now giant-sized shelves filled with books. The first thing to cross her mind was that more than one lifetime would be needed to read them all. But such limitations no longer plagued her.

Andrei had just recovered his breath when he sat down on the western side of the fountain. Then he turned breathless again when he saw the facades of the houses completely covered with paintings, like a colossal gallery wall. He was briefly horrified at the thought that a sudden burst of rain might damage them, but then remembered that there was nothing but sunny skies in that place.

Nada sat on the northern side of the fountain. When she looked straight ahead, her head started to spin. The movie screen blocked out all the buildings in front of her. Indeed, did art films deserve anything less? She wondered anxiously how she could watch them in all of this light, but was comforted by the certainty that it would not do any harm.

Zoran sat on the eastern side of the fountain. He didn't know what the houses on the square looked like, but this was not how he'd imagined them. The buildings were in the shape of musical instruments. An entire symphony orchestra stretched before him. There was no fear of any noise jeopardizing the music. Now that he could see the sounds, he would listen with his eyes and not his ears.

Vesna first decided to make up for what she'd missed on Saturday. All she had to do was think of the book she'd set aside to go to work in the café and it emerged from its place on the bookshelf. It opened up and started to increase in size until it covered all the others. Now her only task was to surrender to the joy of uninterrupted reading in the sunshine.

Andrei knew at once which painting would take priority. Now he realized why the field of poppies had lost its radiance. The artificial lighting had destroyed its spirit and only the sun could bring it back. The painting started to expand too, not just laterally but forward as well, into a new dimension that finally encompassed the bedazzled viewer.

Nada didn't know which film to watch first. She

loved them all equally. How could one beauty be distinguished from another? The order in which she watched them was unimportant. The fact that she no longer had to worry about the cleanliness of the auditorium, the poor attendance, the long trip to work, that was important. Now that she'd been relieved of these trivialities she could truly enjoy herself.

Zoran's eyes could bring any instrument to life. Or all of them at once if he wanted. Later there would be time for orchestral works. First he had to repay his debt to the oboe. During the long days of darkness it had been the only one to offer the comfort of blue. He caressed it with his new sight and his eyes filled with heavenly sounds.

4. The Telephone

WHEN THE TELEPHONE RANG I shot up in my chair. In the still of the night this sudden sound seemed almost like a clap of thunder. Roused out of my reveries, in my initial confusion I could only stare in disbelief at the telephone on my desk, as though seeing it for the first time. The second ring made me snap out of this suspended animation. As I quickly reached for the receiver, almost in fear, I glanced at the lower right hand corner of the monitor in front of me, where four numbers showed the time. That was the only writing on the empty white screen. It was forty-seven minutes after midnight.

I had no idea who could be calling so late. Certainly not an acquaintance, because everyone knows I work at night and no one would want to disturb me. Unless, of course, something had happened that couldn't wait until morning, in which case it surely would not be something nice. Nonetheless, I hoped it wasn't some kind of trouble. Someone had probably dialed the wrong number. That happened every once in a while, although never before at this late hour. Who in the world would think of making a call after midnight? And then pay no attention to the number they'd dialed? People can be so inconsiderate.

I put the receiver to my ear and said sharply, "Hello!"

"Good evening!" said someone at the other end of the line. I'd been certain it would be a young person, most likely under the influence of a substance that had put them in a very happy mood. Instead I heard the deep, serious voice of a middle-aged man, so my hackles came down a little. I'd been ready to deliver a tirade on bad manners to the unknown young caller, but now I just replied, "Good evening," although still in a surly tone.

"This is the Devil," said the man evenly, just like one of my friends saying who was calling.

I sat there speechless for several moments and then hung up the phone. I was ready to understand that someone had called the wrong number in the middle of the night, but to call me intentionally just to play a joke, and an adult to boot! What had the world come to?

The moment I put the receiver down the phone rang again. This time I didn't wait for the idle prankster to say anything, but was quite blunt.

"If you don't stop disturbing me this instant I'll call the phone company and have them put a trace on you. Then you'll have to pay a hefty fine for what you're doing and you might even end up in jail. Aren't you ashamed of such behavior at your age?"

"How can you put a trace on the Devil? If you call the phone company they'll say you didn't have any calls. That would put you in a really tight spot. What could you say to explain the fact that you reported annoying calls that never happened?"

The stranger clearly did not intend to give up. Fine, I had a remedy for that. I slammed down the receiver, which was unnecessary since it couldn't be heard at the other end of the line, but it let me vent my feelings a bit. Then I felt for the button on the back of the phone that turned off the sound and pushed it. There! How convenient. If only it were possible to remove other problems by simply pushing a button. Now how would he be able to continue his nasty game?

I saw soon enough. Or rather heard. The telephone rang again.

At first I thought I hadn't pushed the right button. There are several of them and I don't use them very often, so I might have made a mistake. Letting the phone ring, I picked it up, turned it around, checked which of the buttons turned off the sound and pushed hard, which was also uncalled for since it reacts to the slightest touch. Nothing happened. The sound continued to echo sharply at regular intervals. I pushed the button again quickly another four or five times, with no result. The only possibility I could think of was that the button was broken. What else? I stared at the phone briefly, not knowing what to do. Every new wave of relentless ringing irritated me more and more. I had to do something as soon as possible. So I did the simplest, although not the wisest, thing. I lifted the receiver again, knowing that I was playing into the hands of a crank. Never strike up a conversation with a psychopath because it will lead to no good.

"Listen, you . . ." I started, but the deep voice interrupted me.

"Did you really expect to turn off the Devil with a button?"

When I slammed down the receiver again, I was spurred not only by the same irritation as the first time but also by the icy fingers of fear that suddenly grabbed my chest. I tried to convince myself that it had been easy for him to guess what I'd done because anyone in my place would have tried that first, but this explanation did not seem quite convincing. Feeling a shudder slide down my spine, I promptly got up from my desk, went around it, bent down and with a deep sigh pulled the telephone cord out of the wall socket.

The relief was short-lived. As I was returning to my chair, the telephone rang again. I stopped dead in my tracks, turned around and fixed my eyes on the disconnected cord. I then spent several moments with my eyes riveted to the telephone as it did something it certainly should not be doing. I might have stood there even longer without moving but the ringing seemed to be getting louder each time. Before long the apartments around me would hear it and the last thing I needed was for noise from my study to wake up the neighbors. I had no choice.

I picked up the receiver slowly, waited a bit and then said softly, "Hello?"

"Have you finally come to your senses?" said the same voice reprovingly. "It's simply unbelievable how long it takes people to accept something as innocuous as a telephone call from the Devil. Just imagine what would happen if the Devil himself turned up on your doorstep. Indeed, to be fair, you were quite quick about it, but sometimes it drags on and on. And is unpleasant. Some behave quite imprudently. In their stubborn refusal to confront reality, they sometimes even throw the telephone out the window on the top floor of a building. And then the Devil is to blame when the phone, broken to smithereens, keeps ringing so loudly that it causes panic throughout the neighborhood. But there is no other way. Some people can't be treated with kid gloves."

There was a short lull before I spoke again. My voice was still disconsolate.

"What do you want from me?"

"From you? Nothing."

I hesitated once again.

"Then why did you call me?"

"I was only returning your call."

"My call?" I repeated, flabbergasted, collapsing back in the chair.

"Yes, yours. Didn't you think just a moment ago that you would willingly make a pact with the Devil, anything just so you didn't have to look at the empty screen in front of you? To get some inspiration?"

I swallowed the lump in my throat. I thought of asking him how he knew what had been on my mind, then realized the question was out of place. He probably wouldn't have answered me anyway.

Instead I said, "But that was just figurative . . . metaphorical. I didn't mean it literally."

"Is that so? It didn't look that way to me. Does that mean you don't need my services?"

I had to say right away that I didn't. Even though my heart was pounding wildly and my ears were ringing, I still had enough of my wits about me to reason properly. You should never find yourself in cahoots with the Devil.

When I took my time answering and then said, "I do, but their price—?" it seemed to be coming out of someone else's mouth.

"Everything has its price."

"My soul?" I asked almost in a whisper.

"What hogwash. Who needs a writer's soul? And a failed one to boot."

Although this should have been a relief, it felt like a pin had suddenly been jabbed in my backside.

"Well then, what?" I replied somewhat more forcefully. My wounded pride brought back a bit of self-confidence.

"I'll take great pleasure in your torments."

"What torments?" My voice softened again.

"Mental, of course. What else? You will agonize."

"Oh, that's it." I didn't say anything for a moment, then added reluctantly, "What will I agonize over?"

"What you will be denied."

"What will I be denied?"

"Success during your lifetime or a place in literary history. The choice is up to you."

"I can choose between those two things?"

"Yes. Take your pick. If you want to be considered a great writer in the history of literature, that will be possible, but only posthumously. You will be neglected and opposed during your lifetime. Almost no one will read you. This will make you first wrathful and frustrated, convinced that a great injustice is being done to you. Then you'll start to doubt yourself, you'll slowly lose the desire to write, you'll sink deeper and deeper into despair, and in the end you might even take your own life. Actually, I hope you do. Such an outcome is the best compensation for my services."

"Why would I take my own life when I know that after my death I'll be recognized as a great writer?"

"Are you sure you would find that enough solace? In any case, what kind of guarantee would you have?"

"Our pact, of course. Your word." My voice trembled slightly.

"Many would roar with laughter if they heard that you trusted the Devil's word. Mind you, I always abide by the pacts I make."

"All right, and the other possibility?"

"You'll be very popular. You will be highly read and thereby famous. Probably rich too. Deluded by success, you won't take much notice of the fact that experts refuse to see any kind of literary value in your books. At least not in the beginning. As the years pass, however, this lack of recognition will get harder and harder to bear. The certainty that you will be quickly forgotten as a writer will force you to feel disillusioned, ineffectual, a failure. That will probably not be enough for you to commit suicide—quite a shame, of course—but the suffering will be long lasting."

I didn't know what to reply. We sank into a tense silence.

"That's not much of a choice," I said at last.

"Perhaps, but you shouldn't complain. You at least are able to choose. There are so many writers who are never given the chance to make any kind of choice, even though they call upon me, just like you. Some on a daily basis and some even several times a day. But you can't please everyone, that's clear. Where would that lead us? They are left without success during their lifetime and without a place in literary history."

Something suddenly crossed my mind. "But some writers are successful during their lifetime and achieve a distinguished place in the history of literature. What about them? I mean, what kind of choice did you offer them?"

"None. They simply didn't need my help, so they didn't call upon me. Someone else was their benefactor, unfortunately."

The telephone line went silent once more.

I was the first to break it again. "Do I have to tell you my choice right away?"

"No. You don't have to say a thing about it. I'll have

no trouble establishing what you've decided as soon as you start to write. Everything will be crystal clear."

I sighed. "But that's just the problem. How can I start to write when nothing comes? Would we even be having this conversation if that weren't true?"

"Well, we can solve that problem at least. Write a story about our conversation."

"About our conversation?" I repeated, bewildered. "But I don't write horror stories."

"Is this a horror story?" The tone of his voice seemed tinged with insult and anger.

"No, of course not," I said, hastening to repair the damage. "But you know, the Devil appears. . . ."

"It doesn't have to be literal. Make it figurative, metaphorical."

"It would still be fantasy."

"Do you have something against fantasy?" That same tone of voice.

"No, not at all. I've just never tried it. But, why not? I might give it a crack. . . ."

"There, you see. I suggest that you get right down to work while your impressions are still fresh."

"Of course." I paused. "I suppose I ought to thank you. . . ."

"Don't thank me. Right now this seems like a great service, but in the end you'll curse me for it. And don't call me anymore. It would come to nothing. I only appear once."

"I understand," I replied. "Then, God speed."

I bit my tongue, but it was too late. Before the connection broke, a sound reached my ear resembling a growl, but somehow huskier, more ominous. I hurriedly hung up the phone.

My compulsion for tidiness urged me to put the telephone cord back in the socket where it belonged, but I didn't. It could stay there disconnected, despite the fact that there would be no more unexpected night calls. Even so, when I typed the first sentence of 'The Telephone' at the top of the empty screen—*When the telephone rang I shot up in my chair*—I could have sworn that my ears filled with a sharp, piercing sound.

5. First Photograph

Appearances can be deceiving.

You look at a picture and think you see everything. Young mother with babe in arms. Indeed, what else is there to see? You've seen thousands of such photographs. Even on postcards. It's a cliché, you think.

And yet it isn't. Take a closer look. The two-month-old child (me, although, of course, you can't recognize me on my first photograph) seems intent on holding its head where it's not supposed to be, under its mother's bosom, closer to her stomach.

There's something unnatural about that position. One would expect the baby to long to hear its mother's heartbeat. That's why mothers instinctively hold babies with their head cradled in their left arm.

I suppose I too (although, to tell the truth, I don't remember) loved to hear my mother's throbbing heart. How could it be otherwise? I was a normal baby.

Or perhaps not quite normal. I knew something that, even if I could, I wouldn't have told anyone. Because it wasn't normal. At least not according to the standards of the time. Today people would probably have a different take on it all. Be more indulgent. At least I hope so.

Here, let's check it out. I'll tell you the secret why I,

this weak little baby, was trying with might and main to listen beneath my mother's bosom. I wanted so terribly to hear the beating of another heart that was down there a bit lower.

No, my mother didn't have two hearts. Not at all. Anatomically and in all other respects, everything about her was in perfect order. She certainly would have been horrified to learn about that other heart, particularly since it wasn't hers and yet was located inside her.

Well, all right, whose other heart could that be, you wonder with a certain understandable surprise, in the normal mother of a two-month-old baby?

Here's the answer. The other heart beating in my mother's body belonged to my twin brother. I would like to call him by name, but he was never given one. Not only because he was never born. Had my parents known that he was conceived when I was, they would certainly have had a name waiting for him. As they did for me. But there was no ultrasound at the time.

Wait, wait, I can already hear your interruptions, what do mean to say—he wasn't born? How could he still not be born two months after your birth? All-embracing medicine has yet to record such an event. Without mentioning the fact that your mother, even after bringing you into the world would have been—and looked, which is more important—pregnant.

It truly would have been like that, and your amazement quite fitting, had things taken their natural course. But they didn't. Exactly two months and eleven days after my twin brother and I were conceived, he decided not to be born. It's true we were only fetuses at the time, but you are terribly mistaken if you think such far-reaching decisions can't be made so early on.

All right, not all fetuses are equally mature. Take me, for example. Something like that would never have crossed my mind. I was much more ingenuous. Nothing more far-reaching than enjoying the warm, safe surroundings of my mother's womb interested me. But even then my brother was characterized by a seriousness and responsibility of which few can be proud, among newborns and adults alike.

His decision astonished me, of course. How else could it be? I had counted on us being born together as befits identical twins. How could I enter the world by myself, deprived of the closest relative imaginable? It's not certain I could even consider myself a twin in that case.

Completely distraught, I asked for an explanation. But I didn't get one. All I was told, in the special nonverbal way that fetuses communicate, is that that's the way it had to be. As though Fate itself were talking. It was not until much later that I realized it actually could not have been otherwise. The explanation went far beyond my capacity to understand at that age. It's questionable that I could even today. I sincerely doubt that I will ever reach an understanding of the world to match that of my brother when he was just a fetus.

While I was unable to grasp his reasons for not being born, I wanted to know how he intended to pull it off. This was a technical, not metaphysical question, so I hoped that I would be able to understand it. Was he intending to keep growing and developing in Mother's stomach until he came of age, and even afterward? I was horrified at the thought of what our mother would look like with a grown man in her stomach.

He took me soundly to task for such a vicious thought. Of course he wouldn't keep on growing.

How could he spoil his own mother's appearance? He wouldn't even stay in his current tiny proportions that would certainly cause her no inconvenience. He would go to the opposite extreme. Become smaller.

I must have given him a dumbfounded look with my large fetus eyes, because he hastened to dispel my doubts. Why was I so surprised? We live in an age of miniaturization, don't we? Everything's getting smaller and smaller. We're coming closer to a quantum world in all respects. It turns out that even the cosmos itself isn't quite as enormous as was once thought. So why should fetuses be any exception?

What else could I do but accept this rational explanation. But this did nothing to lessen my concern. When do you intend to start shrinking, I asked him. Sensing fear in my inaudible voice at the possibility of being all alone, he firmly promised that nothing would happen before I was born. He would maintain his current size until then.

And indeed, while I continued to grow, he didn't change. Over time I became so large compared to him that I had to be very careful not to accidentally harm him. Moving about like every lively baby at the end of its term in the womb, I could have smothered him, pressed him or even smashed him.

My anxiety grew as the delivery date approached. It's a tumultuous event, something could go wrong. What if he didn't manage to stay inside? If he came out with me, he wouldn't even be a premature baby. The obstetrician and midwife might not even notice him.

He just waved his bud of a hand dismissively at my anxious questions. I was not to worry, everything was taken care of. He was always to the point when important matters were involved.

He was able to console me in that regard, but not about our parting. It was clear to me that Fate was behind the whole thing, but this didn't make it any easier for me. Is there anything harder than taking leave of your twin brother? It's like parting with your own self. But we're not parting, he assured me. I won't die, I'll just get smaller. And I won't go anywhere. You'll be able to hear my heart whenever you put your ear to Mother's stomach.

Just as he promised, the delivery went smoothly. For both of us. And for Mother too. In spite of her exhaustion, she was cheerful, and everyone misunderstood my cries. They shouldn't be criticized for this, though. Every baby cries at birth. How could they suppose that my tears were from parting with a brother no one knew about?

Although quite weak, ever since Mother first drew me to her breast I made every effort to put my little head on her stomach. At first she found it unusual and brought my head back up, but she got used to it over time. Particularly since I fell asleep the fastest in that position. And what mother wants to have trouble putting her baby to sleep?

My brother's heartbeats, although barely audible, had a calming effect on me. We were no longer touching like before, but we were separated by the very small partition of Mother's skin and a thin layer of fat. You could even say that we were still connected. Just like when we were happily inhabiting the same body.

Well, no idyll is ever of long duration. This one ended when I was four and a half months old. Not all at once, but over three days. At first I thought there was something wrong with my hearing. I had to press my head harder and harder into Mother's soft abdomen to make out the sound of the tiny heart inside.

And then with horror I realized the truth. My brother had set out on the final minimization. At the end of the third day I could no longer hear him regardless of my efforts. And I couldn't try any harder because Mother's stomach had started to hurt from all my pressing, so she held me away from it.

Inevitably I fell ill. Many adults, let alone a baby, would have been crushed by such a trauma. My illness caused the doctors great concern. No one could discover its cause. They examined me thoroughly and tried various therapies, but nothing helped improve my blood count and bring back my appetite. And pull me out of my apathy.

I got better at the beginning of my sixth month. They thought it happened all by itself. The doctors couldn't find the reason for this spontaneous recovery either. But it caused them no concern. Who cares why things are going fine, while they are? They didn't miss a chance, however, to give themselves credit for this favorable turn of events.

And the credit was all mine. I simply started to look at things rationally. At that age a lot of maturing happens in a month and a half, even when you're sick. Or rather, particularly then.

All right, I can't hear my brother's heart anymore, but that doesn't mean, as he himself said, that he died. He's still alive in Mother's womb, he just got smaller. To the quantum level. Maybe even below it. Indeed, miniaturization truly knows not boundaries. And there, as we all know, it's completely immaterial to talk about sound, so there isn't any beating.

This silence from the womb actually came at just the right time. I couldn't keep my head on Mother's stomach forever. What would that look like? Babies have to be weaned sooner or later. It's a bit hard in the beginning, but then they get used to solid food. And start enjoying it.

I rarely think of my brother today. You know how it is: out of sight, out of mind. I only remember him when I look at this photograph, and I don't do that very often. You can't see him, but I know he's there. And I hope he's well wherever he is now. In any case, it was his own choice.

I don't know whether I've convinced you, though. I'd say I haven't. Congratulations on the quantum world, I can almost hear you thinking, but if a person doesn't believe their own eyes, whom will they believe and why? Appearances can be deceiving, but not that much. The picture only shows an ordinary young mother with babe in arms. And since the baby truly doesn't look like me now at this advanced age, how can you believe me when I say it's me? Particularly since my penchant for wild ideas earned me a bad reputation long ago. I'm even trying to make a living out of it.

6. Rendezvous in front of the House

I WAS NOT ASTONISHED when I saw my own self. In my place many people would, naturally enough, have been confused and frightened, but that's only because they have nothing to do with the fantastic. If, like me, they did, they would handle it better. But people prefer to hold onto reality, their feet planted firmly on the ground. Who can blame them for that? They just wave their hand dismissively at the fantastic—all the more so at those having anything to do with it, often mocking, sympathetic at best. Now, this isn't wise. You never know when the fantastic might catch you unawares, so restraint is advisable. Think what you like about it, but keep it to yourself. Don't let it out. As the better-informed know full well, the fantastic holds a grudge. Don't get on its bad side.

Although I was not taken aback, I must admit I was not totally unruffled. Even when you've spent your whole life related to the fantastic, like me, seeing your own self will not leave you indifferent. No such nirvana exists. As you might expect, I got excited. Running into oneself is not exactly an everyday event even for someone well prepared for the fantastic. But the excitement was moderate. I was no more surprised than if I'd come across a distant relative I hadn't seen in a long time.

That's assuming, of course, that I were to recognize him, and with the passing years this no longer happens every time. But I immediately recognized myself, even though one might say it's more difficult. Despite the fact that we are with ourselves every day, we see ourselves less often than we do others. Only in the mirror and in photographs, and then only briefly, unless we happen to be unduly vain. Try to describe your face and you'll see how little you know yourself. Besides, what old man remembers what he was like as an eleven-year-old boy?

To be honest, the recognition certainly would not have been so easy if I'd come across myself out of the blue, particularly since I saw myself with the hood of my slicker pulled up. I could barely see my face under it, and from the side at that. But the encounter was no accident. Not only had I expected it, you might even say that I caused it.

Don't suppose there's anything supernatural in all of this. I'm no psychic or wizard. I think only the worst about such people, by the way. They only sully the honorable name of the fantastic. It has to do with something much more natural and simple, although little is known about it. But for connoisseurs of the serious fantastic it holds no secret. A time-honored truth says that if you spend enough time writing it, in the end the things you write about will start to happen to you.

Well, maybe not everything, that would be too much, and even the fantastic as high art overdoes it—but something, at least. If you are on really good terms with the fantastic, you can even choose what it will be. It rewards its devotees. I took advantage of the fantastic's favor and chose to meet myself. After giving it some thought, I concluded that out of everything I've written, I'd like that best.

I knew the most probable open place to find myself in the past, so I headed there. I was never to be found anywhere else nearly so often as at the front door of the house where I lived from birth until the age of fifty-seven. Except for the infrequent days when I was sick or out of town, I went in and out of it at least once a day. That's where I would have the shortest wait for me to turn up.

That house has many associations for me and certainly deserves a more detailed description, at least from the outside, but this will unfortunately be left out owing to special circumstances that limit this story to 2,000 words. For the same reason there will be no mention of the events that forced me to move out late in life, even though they are exceedingly interesting and gripping. Even tinged with the fantastic.

There is no park across the street from the house, but I used the prerogative of a writer, particularly when they are in their own work, and put one there temporarily, just as long as the story lasts, which won't be long—there, we've just passed the one-third mark. As a citizen well along in years, waiting on my feet, even briefly, would tire me out. It would be more comfortable to sit on a bench, conveniently placed right across from the front door. Furthermore, I looked less conspicuous on a bench than standing in the middle of the street. There is no reason to fear that this adaptation will contravene story rules. We must not be slaves to verity, particularly in stories about the fantastic.

I was dying of curiosity to see how old I would be when I appeared in front of the house. The fantastic had gallantly offered to let me choose this also, but I dithered too long—which can't be held against me, it's not an easy decision—and it ran out of patience and took the matter into its own hands. All I could do was wait there eagerly, but at least I was sitting down.

I hadn't waited long—that's another advantage of short stories—when a boy in a yellow slicker headed up the walk to the front door. It was a bright warm day—otherwise how could I be sitting in a park?—but not the one in which the young boy would stay forever. I remember quite well that it was raining cats and dogs. In general I have a perfect memory of everything that happened that long ago day. And why wouldn't I, since it meant so much to me?

Even if I hadn't seen my little bowed head from the side, I would have recognized myself by that slicker. No one wears them anymore, they can only be found in old movies. It would certainly attract people's attention, but fortunately I was the only one there, even though it is a busy street—that's right, another adjustment, but don't be a nitpicker, everything is still within the bounds of probability. They can be stretched.

The boy's head was bowed because of the rain, but even more because of the turmoil in his heart. He will skip lunch and spend most of that gloomy afternoon and evening locked in his room, stretched out on the bed, staring at the ceiling. He simply won't be able to get the little ballerina out of his head. Only much later will he understand why he'd been unable to chase her image away. That day and for days after, however, he was hopelessly confused, because girls still did not linger in his mind for very long. Particularly not those who were a bit older.

He'd been walking down the stairs from the fourth

floor of the music school where he took violin lessons. He would not have stopped on the second floor where ballet was taught if one of the doors had not been unexpectedly ajar. Music came from behind it and touched something within him. He looked up and down the corridor; it was empty. He crept up to the door and peeked inside.

Outside of his field of vision someone was playing the piano and the voice of an older woman was sharply giving the beat. The ballerina he glimpsed could have been two or three years older than himself. She was wearing a beige leotard and tights, with silver ballet shoes. One hand gripped a bar that ran along a wall lined with mirrors. Her free arm drew a soft arc in the air as she nimbly performed her pliés, doubled by her reflection in the mirror.

He stared at her as though mesmerized. Who knows how long he would have stood there if the sharp voice had not dispelled the magic. Something was not perfect, it had to be repeated. A grimace passed over the oval face framed by long dark hair that was fastened back. Then she turned her eyes to the door and caught sight of him. They gazed at each other for a moment. The very next instant, he raced off. He didn't stop running until he was almost halfway home.

He continued to take the stairs down from the fourth floor because he was afraid of the elevator, but he no longer stopped on the second floor. On the contrary, he quickened his pace. Anyway, there was no reason to stop. Never again did he hear music through a door left ajar.

Great choice! I couldn't have done better myself. What more convincing proof do you need that the fantastic is versed in matters that have nothing of the fantastic about them, and are even of an amorous nature? Well, maybe my long-ago boyish delight doesn't seem like much of a love story, but that's only because I had to give the short version. If I'd had the chance to give it the full treatment, it would have turned into a romantic novel. First-rate. While seemingly unimportant, this event had a profound impact on me. I had many other loves, of course, but the first one is nevertheless unique.

What stopped me, you ask, from going beyond the bounds of this story and writing that novel? There is an explanation, perhaps even an excuse, but it would take more than just a few words, and unfortunately there is no more room here.

Well, I guess that's it. I ran into myself, the fantastic paid me back for the years I devoted to it. I'm happy with its choice. What more could I ask for? As I slowly got up from the bench—it takes longer now than it used to—someone else headed for the house where I lived until 18 years ago. At first I thought it was a passer-by. It was time to put one into the story, otherwise their absence would stretch probability too much. This wasn't some film being shot, causing the street to be closed.

Then I realized it was me again, so I sat back down on the bench. It wasn't over yet. The fantastic had another present for me. I felt flattered. This was certainly no insignificant honor.

Even though I was much closer to my current age—on that occasion, as I quickly recalled, I had been fifty-six—again I recognized myself not by my face but by an object.

Professors have a bad reputation for losing their umbrellas, but I've been using the same big black umbrella since I was twenty-three. Had it been raining, I would have had it right here with me today. It's the only one

I have. I'm not at all bothered by the pitying looks it draws from people who keep up with the fashion. If this were the proper time, I would say something additional about how I got hold of that umbrella—a highly interesting incident, also with traces of the fantastic—but there is less and less space for storytelling; it's not certain I'll be able to fit the story into the given constraints even without the umbrella.

I knew at once which day had come up from the past. There's never a good day to go to the cemetery, least of all when the sky opens up and not even the biggest umbrella can protect you from the downpour.

The professor will first have to change clothes when he gets home because almost everything he has on is wet or damp. Then, as he did once long ago, he will lie on the bed and stare at the ceiling. Since there is no one to call him to dinner, he will stay like that until morning. Immobile, without closing his eyes. The pain caused by the death will be terrible, but it will be cruelly intensified by the realization that this is not just the loss of a loved one, but the loss of his last love.

He should not have let himself get involved with a student. Everything went against that relationship. Strict university regulations, unwritten social considerations, the fact that he was more than three decades older than she. But when has love given any thought to obstacles? Quite the contrary, they only seemed to spur it on. He was intoxicated by his own recklessness, which was out of character and inappropriate for his age.

Not even the intolerable rain could subdue the trembling he felt as he rushed to meet her. Perhaps, if he'd been less excited, if he'd driven with more presence of mind, if the road had been dry . . . Indeed, he had not been found guilty for what happened, officially it was a concatenation of unfortunate circumstances, but was this able to redeem him in his own eyes?

He saw her standing on the curb under an umbrella, waiting for him. She waved and he replied by flashing his high beams. He did not see the old woman until the large dog she'd decided to take for a walk in such rain suddenly pulled her onto the roadway. He would never know whether it was his high beams that frightened it.

The old woman suddenly appeared in front of his car. He could only react by reflex. He hit the brakes and turned the steering wheel sharply at the same time. The car slid to the side and flew onto the sidewalk. At first he didn't realize what he had hit. All he heard was a dull thud.

At the funeral no one held him responsible. On the contrary, they were all kind. The girl's parents, fellow professors and students. It was not until the service commenced beside the grave that he felt a flood of silent accusations pour down on him from under the lowered umbrellas. . . .

Sad indeed, but the fantastic should not be blamed for that. What else could it do? Such was my last love. In any case, there are only two endings for a romance—sad or banal. Would you have preferred the latter?

Don't reproach the fantastic, either, for choosing to revive my first and last loves instead of some happier event. It had duly proposed that I choose which of my former selves to meet. Who's to blame for my dithering?

Very well, now it's high time I got going. The story already has more than 2,000 words and the English translation will be even longer. In addition, the bounds of probability cannot be stretched without end. Finally, the park must be removed as soon as possible so the passers-by who will soon appear don't get confused.

As I slowly rose from the bench, the front door of the house across the street opened. I thought that someone would appear, but no one emerged. A glimpse of the entrance hall was all that could be seen, the rest was in darkness. How apt, I concluded. That's where I'll go. As things stood, I'd been uncertain where to exit the story. True, it looked dark inside, but at least I knew what to expect. I feel right at home in the fantastic.

I crossed the street.

Kissing the Joy

Tamar Yellin

He who binds to himself a joy
Does the wingéd life destroy
He who kisses the joy as it flies
Lives in eternity's sunrise

William Blake

A man runs for a train. What made him late, where he is going and why he is carrying nothing more than his hat and overcoat, we are not told. He is unburdened, free of luggage, and it is this lightness which makes it possible for him to run, to be pulled aboard even, by the obliging conductor. His before and after are irrelevant. And he has no ticket.

"The ticket isn't important. The essential thing is that you made it," the conductor tells him. Above all, we have nothing to do here with explanations. Why the protagonist must give up his hat and coat and shoes, to be placed in a cupboard with myriad other hats and coats and shoes of all descriptions; why he must wear a pair of pink slippers with pom-poms and who is the unnamed She whose stockinged foot the conductor felt compelled to kiss, we do not ask. We simply plunge into the narrative, which like the train, keeps moving.

And what a strange train it is: carpeted and curtained in dark red, lit by candelabra, with six compartments which the protagonist must visit, each in turn. One contains identical triplets eating apples; another, chess-playing monks; the next, a blind painter and a dwarf; the one after that, four girl soldiers with their feet in basins full of water; the fifth, an elderly couple aged ninety and a hundred and seventy-six. We are in the territory of dreams, and of a dream's absurdity. There is something profoundly familiar in each scenario that springs straight from the unconscious.

What does it all mean? You might be tempted to think that Živković is playing a joke at the reader's expense, or more precisely, at the expense of critics who love to seek out symbols and delve for interpretations. Here is a world of totemic objects for them to get their teeth into: a wax button, a horned egg, a wooden dummy, a chocolate basin, a glass corkscrew. A green apple, a black queen, a purple ball, a ladybug, the bars on a prison door. The joke could equally well be at the expense of writers who indulge too much in symbols and riddles. There is even a short quiz at one point, suggestive of those questionnaires with which novelists are sometimes presented by earnest interviewers who demand, like the blind painter, to "see your soul." Only here, Živković gives them the answers they deserve:

"Do you like to trample on young wild strawberries?"

"No, I don't."

"I see. And have you ever dreamed of snails swimming upstream?"

"No, I haven't."

"Aha! Did you ever sneak snowballs into matinée shows at the cinema?"

"No."

"You didn't? And did you ever wonder how many stairs there are in the world?"

"No."

"Interesting."

Of course, the story is much more than this. And while it is a work of joyous humour, that which is laughable in it is also tragic. It gradually dawns on us that our protagonist has been preceded into each compartment by the nameless She, apparently leaving a trail of havoc behind her. The "widow" whose husband sits knitting in the corner of the carriage is consumed by jealousy because he flirted with Her: "Don't pay any attention to him. He's trying to arouse your pity. He expects you to feel sorry for him because he's dead." The monk who lost to Her at chess will be ostracised by the order when it becomes apparent that he must now let his hair grow out. The artist feels driven to tell lies about Her because his relationship with the dwarf is in ruins. And so on. There is pain and dishonesty in every one of these compartments.

Each time, the conductor sets our protagonist straight. She is by no means the author of all this chaos; quite the opposite. But what are the lies and what is the truth about Her? The conductor is in love with Her, that much is obvious, yet we instinctively trust his version of events. She is a woman maligned and defamed as prostitute, wanton, thief and witch. She is a being of immense power, beautiful, brilliant, generous and wise. And, as it turns out, immortal. Is She the embodiment of womanhood, by turns vilified and idealised? Is she the personification of desire? Of mystery? Of comedy? Or is She something altogether more esoteric?

Meanwhile, between each compartment, our protagonist is prepared like a bridegroom for the ultimate encounter: manicured, shaved, teeth scaled and polished, he is measured up for the white suit in which he will go to meet the Beloved. (His pom-pom slippers have been exchanged for a pair of shoes "of very high quality white leather, light and supple.") We might wonder at the personality of this gentleman. One could say he barely has one. He is so amenable as to be passive, so agreeable as to verge on hypocrisy. More charitably, one might observe that his sympathies lie with whomever is pleading their case to him at that moment. He is the perfect blank sheet, the ideal recipient of all that happens to him.

And so he enters the sixth and final compartment, where something transcendent occurs which transforms everything. Wrapped in double darkness, the protagonist is invited to untie his blindfold:

When the blindfold fell off, I wasn't in total darkness as I'd expected. The shapes on the five seats were outlined by a weak glow, as if edged by tiny sparks... The wax button to my right was hexagonal, with a double ring of holes that flickered with a bluish tinge. The horned egg in the middle had two bent protuberances in its lower part resembling stunted limbs, with points that seemed to glow. The wooden dummy next to the window had been pierced at the top, and out of the hole flowed drops of liquid fire. The chocolate basin to my left contained something gelatinous and fluorescent. The glass corkscrew on the seat next to it was periodically suffused with short green flashes that seemed to come from somewhere inside. The last seat in the row was the opaque heart of darkness.

We are almost in the territory of science fiction here, if not of surrealism. Rarely, in fact, have dream, drama, comedy, tragedy and the fantastic been so skilfully combined, and rarely in the service of a dénouement so profoundly satisfying. The "soft, lilting" voice that instructs the protagonist to put the green apple back on the tree ("Apples should be on trees, shouldn't they?"), to stroke the red hair of the black queen ("The queen lit up with joy and ran forward."), to throw the purple ball up into the air ("Don't worry, nothing will happen to it."), to blow on the ladybug ("Ladybugs love air currents.") and to pull apart the bars on a prison door ("It's not at all hard. Try.") is the voice of complete reassurance and total control. It is the power that unfailingly liberates: that of the imagination.

"That is your way out."
"My way out?"
"Yes. Go through the opening."
"Now?"
"Now. Everything has been done."

Isn't the nameless She, after all, the muse of Story, of the relentless narrative that draws us on, providing us, in the end, with the catharsis only a perfect consummation can supply? We feel it in the glow of wellbeing which suffuses the final pages; in the last words of the beneficent She which seem addressed beyond the lovelorn conductor, to the world in general:

"Tell him not to lose hope. That's what is most important."

For Živković, ever the optimist, fiction is an end in itself, the best palliative one could wish for the ailments of living. This brief book is a token laid at Fiction's feet. To the reader who is receptive, it is the fleeting sensation one is left with that makes sense of all the rest. It is a sort of conjuring trick; you hardly know how he has done it. And you don't see how this sublime and ineffable mystery could have been conveyed to you in any other way.

Contributors

About the author

Zoran Živković was born in Belgrade, Serbia, on October 5, 1948. Until his retirement in 2017, he was a full professor at the Faculty of Philology, the University of Belgrade, teaching creative writing.

He is one of the most translated contemporary Serbian writers: by the end of 2021 there were 117 foreign editions of his books of fiction, published in 24 countries, in 20 languages.

Živković has won several literary awards for his fiction, beginning with the Miloš Crnjanski award in 1994 for his novel *The Fourth Circle*. In 2003, Živković's mosaic novel *The Library* won a World Fantasy Award for Best Novella; in 2007 his novel *The Bridge* won the Isidora Sekulić award; and in 2007 he received the Stefan Mitrov Ljubiša award for lifetime achievement in literature. In 2014 and 2015 he received three awards for his contribution to the literature of fantastika: Art-Anima, Stanislav Lem and The Golden Dragon.

Zoran Živković has been recognized with his selection as European Grand Master for 2017 by the European Science Fiction Society at the 39th Eurocon in Dortmund, Germany.

Živković is the author of 23 books of fiction:

The Fourth Circle (1993)
Time Gifts (1997)
The Writer (1998)
The Book (1999)
Impossible Encounters (2000)
Seven Touches of Music (2001)
The Library (2002)
Steps through the Mist (2003)
Hidden Camera (2003)
Compartments (2004)
Four Stories till the End (2004)
Twelve Collections and the Teashop (2005)
The Bridge (2006)
Miss Tamara, The Reader (2006),
Amarcord (2007)
The Last Book (2007)
Escher's Loops (2008)
The Ghostwriter (2009)
The Five Wonders of the Danube (2011)
The Grand Manuscript (2012)
The Compendium of the Dead (2015)
The Image Interpreter (2016)
The White Room (2022)

About the essayist

Tamar Yellin is the author of three works of fiction: *The Genizah at the House of Shepher* was shortlisted for the Jewish Quarterly/H.H. Wingate Prize, was awarded the Harold U. Ribalow Prize and was the inaugural winner of the international Sami Rohr Prize for emerging Jewish writers. *Kafka in Brontëland and other stories* was awarded the Reform Judaism Prize for Literature, was shortlisted for the Edge Hill Prize and longlisted for the Frank O'Connor International Short Story Award. Her most recent book is *Tales of the Ten Lost Tribes*. She lives in Yorkshire, England, where she is a current Fellow of the Royal Literary Fund.

About the artist

Youchan Ito was born 1968 in Aichi prefecture, Japan. She launched her career as a graphic designer in 1988, becoming a freelancer illustrator in 1991 and founding Togoru Co., Ltd. with her husband in 2000. In 2017 the company was reborn as Togoru Art Works. She works with a wide range of genres including cover art and design for science fiction, mysteries and horror titles, as well as illustrations for children's books.

www.youchan.com

www.ingramcontent.com/pod-product-compliance
Lightning Source LLC
LaVergne TN
LVHW051003080826
845145LV00009B/2437

* 9 7 8 4 9 0 8 7 9 3 1 6 5 *